PROUD SURGEON

Tension in the Theatre at St. Antony's Hospital had built up alarmingly during the last few days; Calder Savage, the new Senior Surgical Officer, had really lived up to his name, venting a savage irony on anyone who fell foul of him. But when he gave Staff Nurse Honor Portland a lift home, she was surprised to find what an interesting man he was. Although Calder is generally suspicious of women, he and Honor are drawn together by work and friendship. But can there be more?

Books by Lynne Collins
in the Linford Romance Library:

HEARTACHE HOSPITAL
SWEET INTERLUDE
TREAD SOFTLY, NURSE
THE SISTER AND THE SURGEON
SISTER OF SERENITY WARD

LYNNE COLLINS

PROUD
SURGEON

Complete and Unabridged

LINFORD
Leicester

First published in Great Britain in 1965

First Linford Edition
published 1997

British Library CIP Data

Collins, Lynne, *1933–*
    Proud surgeon.—Large print ed.—
    Linford romance library
    1. English fiction—20th century
    2. Large type books
    I. Title
    823.9'14 [F]

ISBN 0–7089–5034–5

Published by
F. A. Thorpe (Publishing) Ltd.
Anstey, Leicestershire

Set by Words & Graphics Ltd.
Anstey, Leicestershire
Printed and bound in Great Britain by
T. J. Press (Padstow) Ltd., Padstow, Cornwall

This book is printed on acid-free paper

1

HONOR peeled off her mask and her gloves and sighed. She was tired after the long hours under the arc lights of the Theatre, and very thankful that the list was finished. It had been heavy owing to a car crash almost outside the hospital gates and the combined skill and effort of every member of the Theatre team had been called upon to the last ounce to save the lives that had been so nearly lost by careless driving.

Honor was not only tired. She felt as though her nerves had been stretched almost to breaking point. Calder Savage, the new Senior Surgical Officer, was to blame, of course. Tension in Theatre had built up alarmingly during the last few days for he had really lived up to his name, working like a savage but also venting

1

a savage irony on anyone who fell foul of him. And it had not been difficult to fall foul of him for he was in a perverse and finicky mood of late.

The little Honor had seen of the new SSO to date had not unduly impressed her. He had more than his fair share of good looks, it was true, but Honor had never fallen into the trap of judging any man by his appearance. She was a practical level-headed girl who did not give her affections easily, and liked to keep her friendships with the opposite sex on a strictly platonic basis. One day, she hoped, the one man she could really love would come into her life.

So she did not share in her colleagues' excited admiration of Calder Savage and took no part in the eager speculation about him. As a man, he left her unmoved. As a surgeon, she admitted his ability and confidence — and she was in a better position than most to judge these things, for she had been working in Theatre since his arrival at St. Antony's.

Whereas her friend, Joy, was thrilled by his tall good looks, his lithe physique, his slow, delightful smile and his attractively-modulated voice — and the fact that as an unmarried man of thirty-four he was an extremely eligible male — Honor was interested in his skill as a surgeon, his easy and reassuring manner with sick and nervous people, and the fact that he was inclined to be unorthodox in his treatment of certain cases.

During the first weeks in Theatre, she had enjoyed working with him, admiring his skill, and he had proved to be courteous and good-humoured no matter how hectic the pace. She had felt that he was content at St. Antony's and justifiably proud of his skill and they had worked as an excellent team. Because she judged a man by his ability, by his self-control and by the way he worked with his colleagues, she had grown to respect and admire him even while scarcely thinking of him as a person apart from the man who wielded the healing knife.

Now, he was grimly hard to please, demanding one hundred per cent from everyone who worked with him. That was fair and reasonable, of course, and Honor did not deny that it was also necessary when lives were at stake — but she did feel that efficiency could be tempered with amiability. Theatre work was always a strain and the rare degree of informality that existed in Theatre was a valuable asset. It would be a great pity if Calder Savage continued to insist on formality and etiquette in Theatre.

She did not enjoy being barked at as though she were an imbecile and his assistants obviously resented his harsh commands and rough tongue. The anaesthetist was a very important man in Theatre and his word was law. He was in a position to make life very difficult for a surgeon, even the Senior Surgical Officer, if he wished — and he was very likely to wish it if Savage continued to antagonise him with his sarcasm. Theatre Sister could also be very hard to handle at times and a wise surgeon went out of his way to keep on friendly and pleasant terms with her, but the SSO had snapped at her sharply on several occasions and it seemed to Honor that a first-class row was brewing.

She pulled off her cap and shook out her gleaming bronze curls. Her work was almost finished and she would soon be off duty. She thought longingly of a hot bath and clean, fresh underwear and a lazy evening — and realised the utter weariness of her mind and body. She had never felt so tired after a day in Theatre but she had been constantly on edge today.

She wondered if the SSO needed a rest. It was not natural for a skilled surgeon, trained to cope with any emergency, trained to keep a tight rein on his emotions, to be so bad-tempered, so difficult to please, so swift to find fault with everyone and everything, while working in Theatre. Theatre work, for nurses, was very different to ward work. They were allowed to feel that they were human beings rather than the automatons who merely carried out instructions. It seemed odd to consider it so but Theatre often had a somewhat social atmosphere despite the grimness of its work, and Honor had always thought that the easy camaraderie and lack of formality was an excellent safety-valve for tension and urgency and the arduous hours beneath the fierce lights.

It was not uncommon for first names to be used freely and she had even known a flirtation to make rapid progress in such unusual surroundings. The majority of Theatre work was routine and sometimes very boring for the junior assistants, and light-hearted banter was harmless relief for boredom. Calder Savage had taken little notice of it, had even swopped jokes himself with Mr. Taylor and Theatre Sister and Duncan Grey, the anaesthetist, and smiled on the junior nurses with indulgent tolerance. But his caustic tongue had destroyed the friendly atmosphere this week and Honor regretted it very much.

He would soon be the most unpopular man at St. Antony's for he seemed to be setting out to antagonise everyone with whom he came into contact. Was he finding his new job too much of a strain? Was he feeling under the weather and clashing with everyone because he was so determined not to give in to the way he felt? Or was he bad-tempered and perverse and stubborn by nature and not bothering to be pleasant now he had settled in?

Honor shrugged and dismissed him from her mind. There was still work to he done before she went off duty, sterilising instruments, removing waste, consigning gowns and towels and sheets to the laundry basket, leaving Theatre clean and tidy and ready for any emergency during the night.

Before going off duty, she checked that the changing-rooms were empty and tidy — and found a gold signet ring lying beside the wash-basin of the Surgeons' Changing Room. She picked it up, glanced at the engraved initials, the intertwined C and S, and slipped it into her pocket to hand in at the reception desk.

On her way to Main Hall, she saw a familiar figure approaching and spoke to him as he reached her side. "Mr. Savage, were you going down to Theatre? I believe you left your ring in the changing-room." She drew it out of her pocket and offered it to him.

"Thank you. I've only just missed it." He glanced at her indifferently, obviously scarcely recognising her as a member of the Theatre staff.

Honor smiled at him, that exceptionally sweet smile which transformed her rather homely face to beauty if she had but known it. She felt a surprising surge of compassion for him as she noticed the pallor of exhaustion in his face and the strain in his dark eyes. She was not a creature of impulse but unexpectedly she heard her own voice saying with a note of concern: "You don't look at all well, Mr. Savage." She added hastily: "Excuse me, that sounds impertinent."

He turned abruptly and his eyes narrowed as he looked down at her. "Thank you, but I'm quite well . . . just wretchedly tired."

"Yes," she said quietly. "It's been a heavy day."

"It's been a heavy week," he amended rather grimly.

"You'll have the week-end to knit up 'the ravell'd sleave'," she told him, smiling.

"You like Shakespeare?"

She nodded. "Very much. He knows so much about human nature."

"There won't be much opportunity for that 'sore labour's bath, balm of hurt minds, great nature's second course'. I'm going to London for the week-end," he said with a sudden tightening of his lips.

"Then you should be able to forget

all about the hospital for a few days — and that might do you as much good as sleeping," she said practically.

He smiled wryly. "I doubt it. If I had any sense, I'd sleep through the entire week-end and give up the idea of going to town. But I mustn't keep you . . . you're going off duty, I expect."

She nodded and began to walk along the corridor. To her surprise, he fell into step by her side.

"You look a little tired, too, Nurse," he said abruptly. "Are you on duty this week-end?"

"No, I'm free now until Monday morning."

"I don't suppose you'll follow your own advice, though — like every other nurse, you'll be kicking up your heels the moment you're out of uniform. I suppose the young are more resilient and can manage to cope with a series of late nights."

"Possibly we sleep well when we do sleep," she retorted gently.

He looked at her swiftly, obviously

startled by her remark.

"I've had things on my mind," he replied rather defensively.

"I'm looking forward to a lazy week-end," she merely said, thinking it wiser to ignore his remark.

"You're not going home?"

"Home?"

"To your parents — isn't that what most nurses do when they get a free week-end?"

"Oh, yes, of course. But my parents died years ago. I have no family except a brother in South Africa and an extremely bad-tempered aunt who doesn't like entertaining," she said lightly.

"It must be rather dull for you to stay at the hostel every week-end," he commented as they reached Main Hall.

"I'm not living in the hostel," she explained. "I share a flat with a friend."

"I see."

"Well, I must hurry to get my bus now. I hope your week-end isn't as bad as you seem to expect." She smiled up at him once more and turned to leave him.

"Hold on a minute, I'll just speak to the porter and then give you a lift home," he told her firmly. "I've kept you talking when you might have been half-way to your flat."

"But that won't do, Mr. Savage," she said bluntly.

He stared at her in surprise. "Why on earth not?"

"You're the SSO and I'm a Staff Nurse, for one thing. You should know enough about hospital grapevines not to want to give ours food for gossip."

"Nonsense! Do you know my car, the pale green one? It's parked in the quadrangle. I'll join you in a moment. Here's the key!"

Honor caught the key he tossed to her, realised the futility of further argument and passed through the doors as he strode across to the reception desk. It was really very unorthodox, but he did not seem to be a very orthodox person. People would talk even when there was nothing to talk about — and if he wished to drive her home she would be foolish to insist on going on the bus when she was already later than she liked to be. In any case, they had probably provided a certain amount of food for gossip already by walking and talking together in the public corridors of the hospital . . . he obviously had something on his mind, he was a newcomer to St. Antony's and if he found it easy to talk to her, as he obviously did, she might be able to help just by listening.

He did not keep her waiting more than a few moments. He slipped into the seat by her side and turned on the ignition. The car rolled slowly across the quadrangle, passed through the gates and turned into the main stream of traffic.

"I'm assuming that your flat is in the town," he said with a faint question behind the words.

"Yes, that's right. Slater Road, just

off the High Street, the first on the left past the Post Office," she explained.

He turned his head to smile his approval. "Very concise. I shall have no difficulty in finding it."

"It's amazing how difficult it is to reach by bus," she told him. "I can't understand why there isn't a direct route from the centre of town to the hospital by bus; it's ridiculous."

"Isn't there?" he asked carelessly. "Having the car keeps me in complete ignorance of the bus routes, you know."

"I suppose it does, but you don't have to be so smug about it," she said in gentle teasing.

He raised an eyebrow. "Did I sound smug — sorry!"

Honor chuckled. "Sorry, I shouldn't tease you — but you have such an efficient medical air that it's rather surprising that you chose to be a surgeon."

"Meaning that I'm not a good surgeon?" he asked, so seriously that

Honor had to steal a quick glance at his twinkling eyes before she realised that he was teasing her in return.

"You know that you are," she said quietly and without any attempt at flattery.

"Yes, I've been well-taught," he agreed.

"And you have the something extra that every good surgeon is born with," she added.

"You're very kind, Nurse — I must do my best to live up to that generous compliment." He added after a momentary pause to cope with a sudden stream of traffic: "Theatre Nurses are always critical, aren't they? I suppose they have the opportunity to study so many different techniques."

"We are critical . . . but we're also human. We get tired and impatient just like the surgeons — and it helps to have the occasional kind word or smile thrown at us instead of a scathing taunt," she said gently but with an unmistakable implication.

"You've been through the mill this week, I'm afraid," he admitted. "I've been like a bear with a sore head, inexcusable of me, I know. I'm not so very popular at the moment, am I?"

"Frankly, no!"

He smiled briefly. "I'm glad you're honest — my ears wouldn't need to be very keen to hear the mutterings and I'm not so insensitive that I can't feel the knives in my back. Goodness knows I don't mean to take it out on you and the others . . . " He broke off. "Nor do I mean to inflict my woes on you, Nurse," he added, a trifle testily.

"People are never really interested, are they?" she said, smiling. "They always have their own woes to tell the moment you pause to draw a breath."

He threw her a swift, puzzled look. "That doesn't sound very tactful!" he told her reproachfully.

"But it's exactly what you were thinking."

16

"It is, as it happens," he admitted ruefully. He grinned. "You're much too perceptive, Nurse."

"You make it sound like a fault."

He shrugged. "Everyone is jealous of their privacy, you know. It isn't comfortable to be with someone who can read one's thoughts with shattering accuracy."

"I make clever guesses. I can't read thoughts," she corrected. "And I'm not always right, anyway."

"You would be insufferable if you were, and I can't think that's applicable to you."

She was startled by the undeniable hint of a compliment. A faint colour came to her cheeks and to conceal her momentary embarrassment she pointed out the easily recognisable facade of the Post Office.

"Yes, I'd noticed. First on the left, you said?"

"Perhaps you'd care to drop me on the corner, it's only a step from there and it will save you a detour to get back to the High Street. They're trying out a lot of one-way streets at the moment and it's rather confusing."

He pulled into the kerb. She turned to smile and thank him. Before she could speak, he said abruptly: "No, don't thank me. I enjoyed the drive — and your company. Enjoy your week-end, won't you?"

Honor was startled by the hint of envy behind his words, envy of what? Her freedom to do exactly as she liked with her off duty? But surely he was answerable to no one but himself! Her youth and capacity for enjoyment? But he was no more than thirty-five or so — and surely he was not so cynical, so blasé as to feel that life offered no new pleasures for him!

Again acting on a strange impulse, prompted by she knew not what unless it was a compassion for the unhappiness and loneliness she sensed in him, she said hesitantly: "I suppose you wouldn't care to have a cup of coffee with me, Mr. Savage? I really am grateful for

18

the lift — and it's the only thing I can think of to repay you for sparing me the ordeal of the buses."

"I should appreciate some coffee," he said with alacrity and immediately set the car in motion again.

Within a few moments, they reached the big old house which had been converted into flats, one of which Honor and Joy had decided to rent almost a year before. The arrangement was working out very well and both girls appreciated the freedom and the privacy of a flat in contrast to the cramping atmosphere of the hostel.

At the moment of issuing the invitation, Honor had forgotten Joy but as she searched for her key in the pocket of her apron she remembered with some thankfulness that her friend had decided to spend a free afternoon with relatives in a neighbouring town. Joy would have embarrassed Calder Savage with her blatant admiration and interest and, without meaning to spread gossip, would have been unable to check her thoughtless tongue before acquainting the entire hospital staff with the news that the new SSO had visited the flat.

Honor ushered him into the sitting-room. It was a large, comfortable room, not overcrowded with furniture, but pleasant and homely.

It didn't take her long to make the coffee, and she carried it in on a tray, placing it on the low table beside his armchair.

"This is a very nice room," he said as she sat down and began to pour the fragrant coffee. "I've been prowling round — you don't mind?"

"Of course not."

He took the cup she held out to him. "Did you take the place furnished — or are these your own things?"

She smiled. "It's a hotch-potch, I'm afraid — what we could beg, borrow or steal from friends and relatives. Most of it should have been consigned to the junk-yard by now, I suppose — but we're grateful. We were so anxious to get out of the hostel that we took the flat before realising that it would need to be furnished."

"Well, it's a very attractive hotch-potch," he assured her. "I've been looking at your books, by the way."

She looked up quickly, her grey eyes bright with interest. "They are my books, mostly," she admitted. "Joy never sits long enough to get past the first page of a book. I'm a great reader, I just can't resist books."

"What do you read besides Shakespeare?"

"Anything and everything," she said a little ruefully. "I'm not at all conservative — my friends say that I've a head full of useless and inconsequential information." She chuckled. "I expect they're right."

"It's an asset at parties," he said with that faint, humorous quirk of his mouth that she was already beginning to anticipate and delight in.

"Some parties — ours are usually pretty hopeless, I'm afraid. Shop seems to be unavoidable — and you'd be amazed at the fantastic theories that a handful of medical men can produce in the space of a few hours! Students and housemen, overgrown schoolboys for the most part!"

"That's rather harsh," he protested. "I've been a medical student myself — and very touchy they are as a race. Those theories may not seem so fantastic in ten years time when medicine and surgery have taken even greater strides."

"What happened to your theories?" she asked gently.

He smiled and was silent for a moment, reminiscing. "Oh, they weren't so original, they've all been developed by others in one way or another." He paused, then said awkwardly: "I'm sorry, I can't remember your name, if I ever knew it."

"Which I doubt," she capped. "Honor . . . Honor Portland." Her eyes twinkled at him mischievously. "Nurse to my friends."

"You must have an enormous assortment of friends," he said dryly. He sat back in his comfortable chair and leant his head back, eyes closed. His face looked grey with exhaustion, and Honor sat silently for a moment or two before realising that he had fallen asleep.

She was oddly pleased that he should have fallen asleep so naturally. She deemed it a compliment to her understanding and her gift for putting people at their ease.

She sat and studied him thoughtfully. He looked younger and very vulnerable in sleep. He also looked very drawn and she knew that he was on the point of exhaustion. She did not doubt for a moment that he had been sleeping badly at night and she wondered briefly at the cause of his obvious unhappiness. Her innate compassion was stirred and she was hurt by the thought of him struggling with a problem that was evidently not easily solved. Perhaps this week-end in London would solve the matter. Perhaps he would be the self she had come to know and admire and respect on his return. She thought suddenly that she had also come to like him very much in the space of a brief hour. Perhaps because he had been a virtual stranger despite the fact that they had worked in close proximity for some weeks — and now she felt that she knew him intimately.

Impulsively, she wished that she knew what troubled him — and then told herself how unlikely it was that he would confide in her. This was merely an odd interlude in the routine of hospital life. He would eventually take his leave with an apology for his weariness and a murmur of thanks for her hospitality, and when they met again there would be nothing to remind either of them that they had spent a brief hour of their free time together. She would have no claim on his friendship — and it was doubtful that they would ever again exchange anything more than the brief, impersonal conversation of Theatre.

She liked him — but that did not matter. It was nothing more than liking born of compassion for a comparative stranger with a problem. This evening he had wanted something from her — a brief, easy, undemanding relationship in order to forget the thing that was on his mind. She believed that she had supplied it — and she was satisfied.

She wondered how long he would sleep. It was unlikely that Joy would come home until fairly late in the evening so there was no need to disturb him. She rose and softly left the room and went into the tiny but immaculate kitchen. She busied herself with preparing all the ingredients for a quick but adequate meal, interrupting the task only to slip downstairs to the telephone. It had occurred to her that he had probably told the hall porter that he would be at home if needed and she telephoned the hospital to give them her number. There was no need to give her name or address, merely to explain that Mr. Savage was with friends and could be reached without difficulty if it was necessary. It was unlikely as it was his free week-end and he had probably admitted his intention to go to London to one or other of his colleagues — but it was a hospital rule that senior staff should always leave an address or telephone number with the hall porter when going off duty.

She went back to the kitchen and within a few minutes had done all she could. All that remained was to cook the meal, and that would have to wait on her guest's convenience.

He was still asleep when she went into the sitting-room and Honor took a book from the shelf and curled up in a deep armchair near the window. Dusk was approaching and very soon she had to close her book and sit quietly in the gathering darkness. At last he stirred and muttered a name drowsily. Honor thought it was her name and crossed the room to put a hand gently, reassuringly on his shoulder.

"I'm here," she said quietly.

"Heather!" he exclaimed, opening his eyes abruptly.

Honor took her hand away and switched on the table lamp. He straightened in the chair and looked at her blankly, still fuddled by sleep, then he smiled sleepily and said easily: "Is it very late?"

"Ten past seven."

"I've slept for some time."

Honor nodded. "Just what you needed," she told him in her matter of fact way.

"But not very polite," he said ruefully. He looked at her for a long moment. "You should have woken me." He rose stiffly to his feet and eased his cramped limbs.

"You looked too peaceful. I hope you're hungry?"

"Hungry?" He raised an eyebrow.

"Are you?"

"Yes, I suppose so, but . . . "

"I've borrowed an evening paper

from our neighbours — it's there on the table. Occupy your mind while I'm in the kitchen . . . everything's ready but for the actual cooking and that won't take many minutes." She smiled at him and went from the room before he could protest.

He was studying the front page of his newspaper when she returned, and glanced up only to smile briefly.

The smile did not touch his incredibly blue eyes and Honor realised that the brief period of release from his inner anxiety was at an end. With swift understanding, she did not speak to him and he returned to the paper without a word. Honor set the table with her usual calm precision and went back to her cooking.

In less time than he would have believed possible she brought the meal to the table. It was a simple but appetising meal, well-cooked and well-served and Calder ate with every appearance of appetite and enjoyment.

"You're very domesticated — and

a very good cook," he complimented her.

She gave the faint, characteristic shrug of her shoulders which brushed aside the compliment. "Nurses are trained to be domesticated."

"That must be why so many of them get married and leave the profession," he commented.

"Possibly," she agreed. "I think a nurse usually makes a good wife and mother. Several of my friends are happily married and run their homes extremely well."

"And their husbands, I expect," he said dryly.

Honor smiled. "Perhaps they do tend to be ultra-efficient — but that needn't be a bad thing if a girl is intelligent enough to conceal the fact that she manages her husband. Most men do need clever handling, anyway."

"The voice of the expert?"

She coloured slightly. "I was thinking of male patients — and how much easier they are than the women."

"Because of clever handling?"

"Why not?" she countered, a little defensively. "Plus the fact that they are usually nicer and kinder and more patient than women — and never so demanding or critical. When they are really ill they are hardly any trouble — just like children. But they can be difficult when they're on the mend — again like children."

"You don't like nursing women very much?"

"No, not particularly. They hate being ill — and they worry about their homes and their families. Men enjoy being in hospital once they're out of pain — but whereas you'd think that women would appreciate being waited on for a change, they don't really like it very much. They'd much rather do things for themselves and seem to have marvellous will-power. They force themselves to be as independent as possible as soon as possible — and that helps us, of course. But, you know, I'm sure that women look on illness as a weakness, something to be despised on the whole, and their impatience with it naturally rubs off on us."

He listened, nodding agreement, his eyes warm with interest When she broke off, he said quietly: "But you cannot judge men and women by their reaction to hospitalisation, entirely. You may learn something about human nature, I agree — but what about men who are not sick and dependent on your skill as a nurse? Do you think they need 'clever handling', too?"

She glanced at him swiftly, expecting to find the hint of humour quirking his lips. She smiled. "Oh, men are little boys who don't want to grow up," the said lightly.

He raised an eyebrow. "A very sweeping statement. And women?"

"Selfish, unscrupulous and greedy."

Calder laughed aloud. "That's very outspoken." He caught and held her candid eyes. "Do you include yourself in that startling summary?"

Honor nodded. "Of course."

"I wouldn't have thought of you as any of those things," he told her frankly.

Mischief sparkled in her eyes. "If I wanted something really badly I wouldn't worry about anyone who stood in the way — that's selfishness — and I wouldn't be too scrupulous about getting what I wanted — and I'd take it with both hands!"

He wiped his mouth on his table napkin and sat back, a gleam of appreciative amusement touching his eyes. "Such as a man, for instance?"

She was thoughtful for a moment. Then she said slowly: "I'm not sure. I'd rather he wanted me, too, so there'd be no need to be selfish and unscrupulous."

"Naturally, but if he didn't want you — or belonged to some other woman?"

"Then I'd try to forget him," she retorted promptly.

"Denying all your natural instincts?"

"Women don't always follow their

instincts, you know."

"I don't think I do know. I'm not an expert on women," he said with a bitterness that surprised her.

"Is any man?" she asked lightly. "We're rather like chameleons, we adapt ourselves to suit the circumstances. Perhaps that's why men say we're impossible to understand — or perhaps their innate laziness prevents them from bothering to follow the tortuous workings of a woman's mind."

"You've really thought about this business of men and women, haven't you?" he teased. "You're really much too young to know so much about human nature."

Honor glanced at the bookshelves. "I've studied my Shakespeare," she said mischievously.

"Yes." he mused. "But have you really studied people outside the pages of a book. It's impossible to parcel them into neat, labelled categories — and you really shouldn't make sweeping statements. Also, if a mere male may be allowed to say so, you're much too harsh in your judgement of your own sex." He smiled at her gently. "I'll remind you of your views in ten years time and we'll see if you still think the same!"

"I expect they'll be tempered with mercy and charity when I've mellowed a bit," she said, laughing, and left the table to bring in the coffee tray.

He glanced at his watch as she returned. "I've monopolised almost your entire evening and it's time I was on my way."

"You've time for coffee," she said quietly.

"One cup, then I really must be going. I want to make an early start tomorrow and that means a reasonably early night." He took the cup she offered and stirred the contents thoughtfully. "We must do this again, I've enjoyed it," he said easily. "I don't mean that I expect you to entertain me, of course — but perhaps you would have dinner with me one night and

34

we can delve a little deeper into your philosophies."

"I won't come if you mean to laugh at me," she said lightly.

Calder smiled. "No, I won't do that . . . but I'll probably take you up on some of your viewpoints. Would you object?"

"Of course not. No one bothers to take me seriously, let alone explain where I may be wrong," she assured him.

"Then it's time you found yourself a suitable mentor," he told her with mock severity. "Someone older and wiser and with more experience of the world." He drank his coffee and placed his empty cup on the tray. Rising to his feet, he walked over to the window and drew aside the heavy curtains. "It's surprisingly quiet, isn't it, so near the main road. I've just bought a house in Oaklands Drive. Do you know that part at all?"

"Only vaguely. It's an expensive area and most of our friends are as poor as we are," she said lightly.

"Yes, the price was a bit steep but it's a nice house. A bit bare and comfortless at the moment as I haven't had time to furnish it with more than necessities." He broke off, then went on briskly: "However, I really must go!"

Honor went down with him — and, mingled with her reluctance to lose his company, was a sense of relief that he was leaving before Joy came home.

Calder paused on the steps and looked down at her steadily. "Good night, and thank you. We'll meet in Theatre on Monday, of course."

She held out her hand. "Have a safe journey."

He took her slim, well-groomed hand in his own for a moment or two, then he ran down the steps and crossed the pavement to his car just as an open-topped sports car drew up with a squeal of brakes . . .

2

CALDER glanced back at the house as he drove away but only saw a strange girl looking down the road towards him. The friend, he assumed, and wondered if she had recognised him from the brief glimpse she must have had of him. It did not matter very much if she had.

Honor was a nice, straightforward girl, he mused, as he tangled with the traffic in the High Street — not outstandingly attractive but with really lovely eyes and a very sweet smile to redeem the homely looks. He had never found it possible to think of any woman as nothing but a friend before, but then he had never known any woman quite like Honor Portland. There was something very refreshing about her complete lack of foolish sentiment in her dealings with him.

He thought with a faint stirring of pleasure that she might prove to be an excellent friend — one who would make no demands on him and would appreciate that there were times when he needed her company and times when he scarcely gave her a thought. He had always believed that such a relationship could only exist between men, but there was nothing masculine about his gentle hostess, despite her practicality and quiet common sense.

He was very grateful to her. For a few hours, he had felt that a burden was lifted from his spirits — and he felt refreshed and more able to cope with the week-end that lay ahead. It did not take him long to reach the other side of town and the quiet, tree-lined road with its pleasant, detached houses.

His footsteps echoed hollowly in the uncarpeted hall as he crossed to the room he had more or less furnished as a sitting-room cum study. For the time being, he was looking after himself but he knew that he must soon advertise for a housekeeper. He had intended to leave such domestic matters to Heather, now he must attend to them himself for Heather would probably never live in this house.

It had seemed that everything was coming right at last — which just proved how wrong one could be! It had been a marvellous stroke of luck to secure this job at St. Antony's: he liked Camhurst, the progressive but friendly town which housed the hospital; for the first time since taking up medicine as his career, he was in a position to marry, buy a house and settle down to a happy and comfortable way of life.

His trust in Heather's love and patient loyalty had been implicit. He had been so sure that she would be content to wait until he had established himself firmly as a surgeon and could offer her all the things they had so often dreamed about and discussed. It was eight years since they had met and fallen in love; eight years since he was a medical student and she was a junior student nurse at Bennet's. Eight years of loving and waiting and dreaming — years in which he had stifled his longing to marry the girl he loved and worked and studied to be in a position to marry; years in which he had been able to rely on her understanding and her loyalty and her patience and the knowledge that she would marry him as soon as it became possible.

Now he was a fully-fledged surgeon with a plum post — and Heather was a Sister at a suburban general hospital on the outskirts of London.

During the few short weeks that he had been in Camhurst, he had scoured the town for a suitable house for his bride. He had spoken confidently to his new colleagues of his intention to marry In the near future and, knowing the grapevine that so efficiently worked in any hospital, did not doubt that it was common knowledge from the Board of Directors to the merest ward maid by this time. He had written long, loving letters to Heather, describing Camhurst and the house and the hospital and pouring out his plans for the future and his thankfulness that now, at last, they could be married.

Then, like a bombshell, he'd received her letter — and his whole world had toppled. Even now he remembered every word written in her neat, distinctive handwriting on the blue notepaper she always used — the contents were still searing his brain and his heart.

Heather was extremely reluctant to hurt and disappoint him but she really did not feel that she could marry him, after all. It was eight years since they had met and during their long and somewhat cool courtship both had matured and changed a great deal. She was sure he would understand that she could not help the way she felt and she hastened to assure him that her decision had nothing to do with any other man. It was merely that she had no inclination towards marriage at all at this stage in her career: she was happy in her job and ambitious enough to agree with him that a career came before personal feelings — an ambiguous comment that had brought the first surge of anger to replace the incredulous dismay; she wished him every success at St. Antony's and hoped to hear at a later date that he had found happiness with someone who was more suited to him.

The finality of which had convinced him that Heather had long since ceased to care for him and had merely lacked the courage to admit it until now.

Calder buried his head in his hands. He was a proud and sensitive man and Heather's letter had been a shattering blow to his pride and his heart.

He could scarcely believe it even now. There had never been any indication that Heather's feelings for him had lessened or altered in any way. That letter was so cold, so stilted, so unfeeling — not in the least like his lovable, warm-hearted, generous Heather who had waited without complaint or reproach for so many years. What did she imply by that reference to their 'somewhat cool' courtship — that he had been lacking in warmth and affection and concern? It was true that he had kept a tight rein on his feelings when they were together, knowing it might be years before they could marry, not wishing to make things any harder for either of them by a display of the ardent and passionate desire that so often consumed him. Had Heather really construed restraint as coldness? Was it possible? Surely she had always known how deeply he loved her, how much he wanted her, that she was his lodestar in life?

That cold, cruel letter could never have been penned by the girl he loved. Heather had never been afraid to face facts, never shown herself a coward in any circumstances. It was just not like Heather to hide behind the safety of a letter rather than face him with the truth that she no longer loved him and did not wish to marry him.

But it was her handwriting — that neat, careful script which had always delighted him so much. And it was her notepaper, specially embossed with her name in gold letters on the pale blue background — a fancy about which he had always teased her. And while the words were formal and stilted and heartless, her own inimical style of writing had crept in from time to time.

Anger swept through him once more. Heather must have known for some time that she did not want to marry him. Why had she allowed them to drift without making her change of heart clear to him? Why had she strung him along with implied promises and constant references to their future marriage? Why had she changed her mind at all?

There had been no hint of this shattering of all his hopes and dreams at their last meeting. It was true that she had not shared his reluctance to put so many miles between them — but he had construed it as a natural interest in the furthering of his career. She had encouraged him to apply for the Camhurst post and mentioned how much easier it was to find a house in the Midlands than on the outskirts of the capital. She had even talked of working at St. Antony's with him for a while after their marriage, if the hospital accepted married staff. Was it surprising that Calder had come to Camhurst in the confident belief that he would soon be a married man and immediately set about finding a suitable house in the vicinity?

Curse her! Curse all women! How dared she do this to him? He had worked hard and long with only one thought in mind, their eventual marriage and the provision of security and comfort for his wife. His success had suddenly turned to ashes in his mouth. Was it for this he had thrown up a good job at Brook's, relinquished a comfortable and convenient bachelor flat and the advantage of being within an hour's journey of Heather to come to a shabby little town and a hospital which was old-fashioned and virtually unknown? In time he could have made a name for himself at Brook's, become a consultant surgeon with rooms in Harley Street, moved in the best circles and met with respect and deference on all sides. But, thinking of Heather, loving her and wanting her, feeling that they had waited long enough for their happiness, he had applied for this job at St. Antony's and secured it in the knowledge that while he might never be famous as a surgeon, might never reach Harley Street, might never become a respected and valued consultant with raw young medical students hanging on his every word, at least he could marry Heather and keep her comfortably and settle down to married life and the possibility of children, without financial anxiety.

It just didn't make sense! There had never been the slightest doubt in his mind that Heather loved him — or that she was not content with their strange and difficult courtship. Now, completely unexpected, a bolt from the blue, came this wretched letter breaking their engagement — and hoping that he would find happiness with some other woman! That last tactless comment made his blood boil! Did she expect him to rush into the arms of the first woman who came his way? Did she imagine he was completely without feelings — or didn't she care that the bottom had dropped out of his world without warning? He was darned if he'd ever make such a fool of himself over a woman again, as if the woman existed who could compensate him for the loss of his lovely Heather.

As soon as he'd finished reading the letter, he'd picked up the telephone receiver with a grim expression in his eyes and given the switchboard operator a London number.

It seemed an eternity before he was through — and another before he was finally connected to Heather's ward.

He fumed with impatience while her Staff Nurse hurried to call her to the telephone but at last Heather's quiet, efficient tones sounded in his ear. His heart leaped at the sound of her voice and for a moment he found it impossible to speak.

"Hello? This is Sister Jennings. Who is that?" she said again.

"Heather, it's Calder."

"Oh!" There was a brief pause and then she went on a trifle unsteadily: "You know I'm not supposed to take personal calls while I'm on duty, Calder. Can't you ring me at the flat this evening?"

"This can't wait," he said with some asperity.

"Then please make it brief," she said quietly. "I'm in the middle of doctor's rounds."

"This letter . . . " He broke off, bit his lip and went on again harshly: "This ridiculous letter — what the devil does it mean?"

"I did try to make it perfectly clear,"

she said hesitantly. "It wasn't very easy to write, you know."

"Do you think it was easy to read?" he snapped grimly, more consumed by anger than any other emotion at that moment "Look here, Heather, you can't just write a letter and expect me to accept that as the end of everything I've wanted for more years than I care to remember. I won't accept it — not till I've heard it from your lips and seen it in your face. I'll be in London this week-end and I want to see you."

"I'm on duty this week-end," she protested and he fancied there was a faint note of panic in her voice.

"Not for the entire forty-eight hours," he told her cuttingly.

"Well, no, of course not, but . . . "

"Don't you think you owe me something, Heather? Don't you think I'm entitled to an honest explanation of this letter?"

"I tried to explain . . . "

"Well, it wasn't a very satisfactory explanation — you'll have time to

49

think of a more convincing one by the week-end. You'd better get back to the ward — I'll ring you when I get to town."

"I don't know that I want to see you, Calder," she said firmly and he knew that she was annoyed by the tone he had taken with her.

"I don't suppose you do, my dear — but I insist on it. Breaking our engagement by letter was an insult that I just won't stomach, and it astonishes me that you could do such a thing. We'll talk about it at the week-end. Good-bye!"

He slammed the receiver into its cradle — and wished that he had not made that call. It had served no good purpose. If she resented the way he had spoken — and he did not doubt that she did — then she was not likely to meet him with a very good grace; and how could he hope to patch up whatever rift lay between them with such a poor beginning? He had lashed her with his sarcasm, scarcely allowed her to speak and flaunted his hurt pride rather than his shattered feelings. It had been a mistake to telephone her, and it would probably be a worse mistake to drive all the way to London to see her at the week-end, but he had insisted on seeing her and he was determined that she should tell him to his face that she no longer loved him, no longer wished to marry him, no matter how much it might lacerate his feelings . . .

He came back to the present with a start, unaware of how long he'd been standing, thinking, in the almost empty room. He stooped to switch on a bar of the electric fire. The house was cold and empty and cheerless — and he compared it fleetingly with the flat he had so recently left. A pleasant fiat, the furniture a little shabby but comfortable, a homely flat with the little touches that made it a home rather than just a place to live. Which was all that this house was or ever would be, he thought grimly as he crossed to the sideboard to pour himself a drink. Only

Heather's presence could make it home for him.

Once he knew definitely that Heather would not marry him, he must decide what to do about the house. He would certainly get the same price for it that he had paid, if he decided to sell. He would be more comfortable and it would be more practical to sell and move into a flat. After all, it was a form of masochism to live in a house which had been bought for his bride. At the same time, there was a remote possibility that he might wish to marry someone else one day in the distant future . . . and a house such as this would probably cost twice as much by that time.

It would not be so bad when it was furnished and the decor and been altered to his liking, but how much time was he likely to spend within its walls, anyway? It was a place in which to entertain and he supposed he would do a certain amount of entertaining. A man in his position had social obligations, a man in his position really needed a wife, not only from a personal point of view but also to act as a hostess on social occasions. There were men who managed without a wife and he was probably destined to join their ranks. For he simply could not visualise a time, even in the very distant future, when he would want to offer marriage to any other woman.

Heather was all that he had ever wanted. His lovely, delightful Heather with her enchanting beauty, her elegance and self-possession, her quick vivacity and striking personality. He had always delighted in her. He and always been thrilled and proud to be with her, conscious of the glances of admiration for her and envy for him, more than a little possessive because she was so beautiful that men were instinctively drawn to her.

He had never doubted her love or her loyalty. Now, with the taste of bitterness in his mouth, he wondered if he had been too trusting, too complacently sure that he was the one man she wanted. He had been so confident that she loved him, it had scarcely occurred to him that she could fall out of love with him or that another man could attract her, even for a moment.

Soon he would know the truth — for if he gained no other satisfaction from his trip to London he was determined to hear the truth from the woman he loved and wanted so desperately.

He did not sleep well, tired though he was, but he was getting inured to bad nights and felt comparatively fresh when he set out for London the following morning.

The roads were busy and the journey took nearly twice as long as he had anticipated. By the time he reached the outskirts of the capital, his temper was frayed and he stopped at a roadhouse for a stiff drink and a meal.

He was trying not to think about Heather too much for apprehension rose in his throat and his stomach muscles tautened uncomfortably whenever she crossed his mind. He forced himself to think about St. Antony's, the operations he had performed during the past week, the friendliness of Honor Portland, but that was a mistake for she inevitably reminded him of Heather. Not that she was anything like Heather in looks or personality or manner, but she was a woman and he was in the habit of automatically comparing other women with Heather, usually to their disadvantage.

He drove to the suburb which housed the general hospital where Heather worked, booked in at an hotel for the night and then telephoned to let her know he was in the vicinity. An impatient Staff Nurse informed him that Sister Jennings was off duty and Calder replaced the receiver on a murmur of thanks and the assurance that there was no message. A slight frown touched his eyes. Heather had assured him that she would be working over the week-end; it was possible that she was off duty for a few hours and might be at her flat.

He left the hotel, nervously straightening his tie and brushing the crisp dark hair back from his temples, and drove as quickly as traffic would allow to Heather's address.

Outside the house, owned by the hospital and converted into flats for senior staff, he sat behind the wheel of his car for a few moments, mustering his arguments and persuasions. He wished he could feel angry with her but he was only conscious of apprehension and a despairing lack of confidence. His anger had died in him days before leaving a bitter, aching disappointment and frustration, he could not whip it to life now. It would not be easy for him to plead with Heather — but his happiness depended on how successfully he could swallow his pride.

Abruptly he got out of the car, ran up the steps and into the house. It would be an anti-climax to find she was not at home. He kept his finger on the bell-push for a seeming eternity before the door eventually opened.

Heather, with tumbled hair and slim body wrapped in a dressing-gown, looked at him for a long moment, and there was an expression in her eyes that he could not analyse. But he recognised the reluctance with which she held the door wider and moved for him to enter.

"You'd better come in," she said quietly.

"Thank you." He spoke stiffly, hurt by the shade of indifference in her tone. "I hope I haven't called at an inconvenient time?"

"I was just about to have a bath," she explained. "Sit down, Calder I must go and turn off the taps."

Heather hurried from the room and he remained on his feet, glancing about the familiar room, unconsciously seeking some proof that the had given her affections to some other man. But there were no photographs in evidence, no huge bouquet of flowers that she might have received from a man.

Conscious of embarrassment and a slight guilt, he turned hastily as she came back into the room, slipping pins into the mass of hair that she had hastily bundled at the nape of her neck. He thought with sudden tenderness that the untidiness of her gleaming hair had divested her of the self-possession she desperately wanted to convey — and he realised that she was as embarrassed, as nervous, as awkward as himself.

"I didn't expect you so early," she said with an attempt at lightness. "You must have left Camhurst at the crack of dawn."

"I tried to get in touch with you at the hospital," he said.

"Did you?" Faint colour stole into her cheeks. "I suppose you were told that I'm off duty this week-end?"

He glanced at her quickly. "A sudden change of plans?" He didn't want to think that she had deliberately lied to him earlier in the week.

Heather gave a faint shrug. "It might have been difficult for us to meet if I'd been working," she returned cautiously.

"Then you did want to see me?" he countered impulsively.

"Of course. My letter didn't seem to make much impression on you. I thought it would be less painful for you that way but if you insist on talking about us there isn't much I can do about it." She was restless, moving about the room, straightening a cushion, toying with an ashtray. He thought that she had never looked more beautiful . . . her red-gold hair gleaming in the bar of sunshine that fell across her at that moment, a few bright curls escaping from the pins to nestle on her neck, the faint warmth of embarrassment touching her cheeks and the sweep of her thick lashes as she lowered her eyes abruptly from his gaze. Those hazel eyes were very wary and he was puzzled.

"I've missed you," he said abruptly.

"You can't have been very busy," she retorted with faint mockery. She smiled at him then but it was a slightly scornful smile with none of the warmth and affection he had come to expect as his due. Deeply hurt, shaken by the complete lack of feeling in the woman he loved, he caught her by the shoulders in a grip that must have bruised.

"Why, Heather, why?" he demanded fiercely.

She did not struggle beneath his strong hands. She looked at him steadily for a long moment. "It's just finished," she said quietly and almost hopelessly.

"I don't believe it," he protested with the anger of despair.

"You have to, Calder, it's too late. I just don't want to marry you now.

He released her as swiftly as he had gripped her. "Did you ever?" The words held a deliberate sneer.

Her eyes held reproach and her hands moved instinctively to refute his words. But she controlled her feelings and her voice was still steady and perfectly calm as she replied: "Yes, very much at one time. I think you must know that, Calder."

"I'm sorry."

She gestured to dismiss the apology. "Never mind — you're upset. This wasn't a good idea, you know. I didn't want you to come to town. Why couldn't you have accepted my explanation and left it at that?"

"Because I love you!" The words were fierce. "I've always loved you. Why in heaven's name don't you want to marry me? Why the sudden change of heart? A month, three weeks ago, you were thrilled that at last we would make proper plans for our future! Your letter was a complete mystery."

Heather broke into his accusing tones. "I thought it was reasonably clear. I told you that I wasn't going to marry you and I gave my reasons."

"Reasons?" He almost snorted with disgust. "That you happen to like being

Ward Sister at a suburban hospital too much to give it up for 'personal feelings'? Rubbish! I gave you credit for more intelligence than to imagine that weak excuse would serve to convince me of anything!"

"I do like the job — very much. I'm very happy at the moment, it's a well-run hospital and I have an excellent staff on my ward. But I didn't mean to offer that as an excuse, Calder. You misunderstood me. I obviously made the mistake of trying to explain too much — I should have kept my letter brief and merely told you that I no longer love you and therefore cannot possibly marry you."

"I just don't understand," he said slowly.

"I didn't really think you would," she retorted with some asperity. Impatiently she brushed back a wing of her hair. "I can't make it any clearer without being brutally frank, and there isn't any point in hurting your feelings."

"My feelings! Good grief, Heather,

what kind of hell do you think I've been through this week? And you talk about hurting my feelings at this point!" He stubbed his cigarette angrily. "Be brutally frank if you think it necessary. I'll take care of my feelings."

Heather spread her hands helplessly. "Calder, this is hopeless," she remonstrated. "We're at loggerheads — we just can't discuss anything when we're both on the point of losing our tempers. Why did you have to force the issue so soon?"

"It may seem premature to you but I've been waiting all week to straighten this out and I'm not in any mood for social chit-chat until you feel it's the right moment!"

She sighed. "Very well. What do you want to know? Why I don't love you now? I can't explain . . . it just died on me. Is there another man? No, there isn't — I told you that in my letter. Will I change my mind again? Most unlikely. We've outgrown each other, Calder — and we've grown away from each other. Haven't you felt it?"

"Cut and dried," he said with emphatic anger. "That's exactly what infuriated me about your letter — so positively cut and dried, indifferently dismissing something that's been vitally important to me — and, I thought, to you — for over eight years? Your love just died on you," he added contemptuously. "Am I to accept that without a word of protest? Would you have quietly faded out of my life if I'd told you that my love for you had just died on me? It isn't good enough, Heather! You have to have a reason. I must have disillusioned you, disappointed you, done something to kill the way you felt about me."

"You did," she said bluntly.

He was taken aback. The words had tumbled from him so rapidly that he had not paused to think whether or not they were really applicable. "In what way?" he asked, a nerve jumping at the corner of his mouth.

"You made me wait . . . and

wait . . . and wait!" she flared. "I'm flesh and blood, Calder I wanted to marry you, I wanted to have your children, I wanted our happiness years ago not at some distant date when you felt it was right to get married. I'm sick of being thrust aside for your work, your career. I know it's important, I know how you feel about it — but I wanted to feel that I came first whatever happened. And I didn't — I never have! Your kind of love might suit some women, it isn't good enough for me! Eight years, and nearly all of them wasted as far as my life is concerned. Oh, not your life, not your career — you're on the way to getting what you want! I only wanted you, and now I don't — it's as simple as that!"

He was very pale and very tense, shocked and bewildered by the torrent of emotion, by the revelation of feelings that he had never suspected.

"Why did you never tell me the way you felt?" His voice was low, despairing.

Heather shrugged. "I've tried — a dozen times at least. Every time you gave me the same old arguments against getting married — you couldn't really afford it at that particular time, your job was very demanding and you wouldn't be able to give up as much time as you'd like. Mr. Burnley didn't like his house surgeons to marry because their work usually suffered, houses were expensive and flats impossible to find, it was more sensible to wait until you were really established. For heaven's sake, Calder, even you must realise the emptiness of those arguments. You could have married me six years ago, there wouldn't have been much money but I could have continued to work — it wouldn't have murdered your pride! I knew and appreciated the demands of your job — did you really think I'd resent them? For my part, Howard Burnley could have disapproved as much as he liked — but if I'd been a house surgeon under him and wanted to marry I wouldn't have given a fig for his opinions. You were a good houseman, Calder Do you think he'd have put obstacles in your path to promotion merely because you'd married against his wishes? We'd have found somewhere to live, if I'd scoured the streets of London all day and all night, and it wasn't really very sensible to wait so long that the thing we were waiting for gradually became unimportant to both of us!" Angrily she ran a hand over her wet eyes.

"It's still important to me," he said quietly, not knowing what else to say. Her tirade had left him without defence for in all fairness he had to admit the truth of her words.

"Is it? Or is it just habit?" She threw the question at him fiercely.

"I love you, Heather."

"That's habit, too," she snapped angrily.

"No . . . "

"Do you think I don't know? Do you think I haven't faced the truth for myself? Don't you understand now why

I won't marry you? My love was worn out years ago, worn out with waiting. I continued to think I loved you because it was a habit and nothing else. We're not even compatible, Calder," she went on wearily. "We don't think alike, we don't want the same things. You're eaten up with ambition, and all I want, all I've ever wanted, is a husband and a home and children. And that's something you don't even understand! Everything in good time — that's your motto, take what you want while you still want it — that's mine!"

Calder looked at her with helpless resignation in his dark eyes. "There doesn't seem to be anything I can say, Heather. You were right, I should not have come. It was a pointless journey."

He moved towards the door — and instinctively she put out a hand to stay him. "No, don't go like that, Calder," she said impulsively. "Not hurt, angry — that isn't the way I wanted it, believe me."

He looked down at the slim fingers resting on his arm, gripping him with urgency. For a moment he covered her hand with his own. "I'm not hurt — or angry, darling," he reassured her gently. "Just completely at a loss."

"I lost my temper, it doesn't do any good. I've hurt you — I've explained things so badly . . . "

"On the contrary, you've made things very clear," he said with a trace of grimness.

"Don't rush away," she pleaded. "Let me make some tea. Sit and talk to me for a little while. Surely we can be friends, at least? I am fond of you, Calder."

A travesty of a smile touched his mouth. He stood looking down at her, hurt beyond words, hopeless and helpless in the face of her indictment — and completely unable to deny the plea in her hazel eyes and flushed, uplifted face.

3

HONOR walked slowly home from church. She was disconcerted to find that the simple service had not calmed her as she'd hoped it would — her thoughts were still on the events of the evening before last.

What a strange man Calder Savage was, she thought, so full of unhappiness and bitter feelings.

She remembered Joy's reaction to his visit. Her flat-mate had come bursting in with her usual exuberance . . .

"Wasn't that the SSO?" she demanded without pausing for breath as she caught Honor on her way out of the living-room with the coffee tray.

Honor had not lingered on the doorstep once she recognised the occupants of the sports car and, by appearing preoccupied, she hoped to escape Joy's questions. But she should have known that Joy would not rest until she had the entire story.

"The same," she returned dryly, realising the futility of denial. She went past her friend and into the kitchen.

Joy followed. "But what was he doing here? He was here — I saw you talking to him!"

"You may believe the evidence of your eyes. He was here," Honor said dryly. "He brought me home, came in for coffee and didn't seem in a hurry to leave," she added tersely, not wishing to be drawn into detailed explanations.

"Well!" Joy stared in amazement. "You are a dark horse! How long has this bee-utiful friendship been going on?"

"You have a nasty, suspicious mind," Honor said lightly, stacking the dirty dishes and running hot water into the sink. "I was late. He offered me a lift and I accepted — and it's the first time

I've discussed anything but shop with him since he came to Camhurst. Any more questions?"

"No need to be touchy," Joy said irrepressibly. "I'm just surprised, that's all. He's been an absolute pig all week and upset everyone with his beastliness — and yet he goes out of his way to bring you home and be nice to you."

"How do you know it was out of his way?" Honor countered, busying herself at the sink.

"Don't be so literal! You know what I mean — and it was, anyway. He lives in Oaklands Drive and that's the other side of town," Joy retorted. "You must admit that it's very odd, ducky. He's been distinctly offhand with every female who crossed his path — and now, with suspicious rapidity, he's making a play for you! What have you got that the others haven't, I wonder?"

Irritation surged but Honor suppressed it resolutely. It would be a mistake to

72

encourage Joy to suppose that there could really be any emotional interest in her brief encounter with Calder Savage.

"Don't make a big thing out of it, Joy," she said calmly. "Perhaps he felt like company — and I just happened to be at hand. He hasn't been in Camhurst long enough to have made many friends, after all."

"He seems to have made one out of you without much effort and in a surprisingly short space of time," Joy returned slyly. Honor made no answer. Her friend gave a quick glance about the kitchen. "You've even fed him," she said with faint accusation.

"Naturally. We were talking and the time slipped by and I had to eat so I invited him to join me."

"Just like that!"

"Yes, just like that," Honor agreed with calm and infuriating indifference.

Joy stared at her suspiciously for a moment, then she shrugged her slim shoulders.

"Are you going to see him again?" she asked curiously.

"I see him almost every day in Theatre," Honor replied carelessly.

Joy slipped out of her coat. "Don't be obtuse, ducky. I wish I'd been in your shoes! He wouldn't have left without making a definite date with me, I know!"

Honor could have told her that the reason why her popularity with men had never brought her an engagement or wedding ring lay in her obvious interest and eagerness to turn a casual affair into something more serious and lasting. But she wisely did not say anything of the kind, knowing that it was something that Joy would have to learn for herself.

"Does he know that you're off duty this week-end?" Joy challenged.

"It was mentioned," Honor admitted, stacking wet dishes with unnecessary care. "Why?"

Joy ran her fingers idly over the draining-board. "I just thought he might have asked you to go out with him, that's all."

"He's going to London this week-end."

"Is he? To see his fiancée, I suppose." Joy threw the remark carelessly at Honor, but kept an observant eye ready to note any reaction.

Honor was startled but determined not to betray it. "Quite probably. Do you want some coffee, Joy? There's some in the pot and it should be hot, still."

"You knew he was engaged, of course?" Joy poured herself a cup of coffee, still watching Honor beneath the thick veil of her lashes.

"It isn't really surprising, is it? Most men of his age have attachments of one kind or another," Honor countered lightly.

"He's getting married within a few weeks. That's why he bought that big house on Oaklands. Why do all the attractive men have to be out of bounds?"

"It doesn't seem to prevent some girls from casting out lures whenever the opportunity arises," Honor retorted dryly.

Joy chuckled. "Meaning me? But the opportunity doesn't arise very often, not while I'm stuck on a medical ward. A woman's ward at that! Anyway, there aren't that many attractive men floating about St. Antony's — attached or otherwise. I do think it's a pity that Calder should have tied himself up before coming to Camhurst. She's a nurse, you know, a Ward Sister at some hospital near London."

"You have an amazing talent for picking up information," Honor told her lightly.

"Oh, everyone knows he's getting married, that's why I was surprised at his interest in you."

"He isn't interested in me," Honor retorted swiftly.

Joy raised a sceptical eyebrow. "He held your hand long enough on the doorstep."

Honor laughed involuntarily. "Is there anything you don't see, Joy?" she demanded mischievously.

Joy grinned. "Not much, anyway. I'm very observant, even from a distance."

"Well, you can dismiss the idea that Mr. Savage is interested in me," Honor said firmly. "A man in his position, with marriage in the near future, isn't likely to risk stirring up gossip by starting an affair with a nurse at St. Antony's. His manner with me was completely impersonal — and I wouldn't have wanted it any other way." She dried the last dish and began to tidy the kitchen. "Do you intend to discuss Calder Savage for the rest of the night — or may I have a bath and go to bed? It's been a long day and I'm tired."

Without waiting for a reply, she went from the kitchen and crossed the hall to the bathroom.

The hot, scented water eased away the stresses and strains of the long day and Honor relaxed and allowed her thoughts to drift drowsily.

It had been easy to talk to Calder Savage, easier than she had expected, for even when he had been polite and pleasant in Theatre in the early days, she had sensed his reserve and reticence and decided that he was not the type to reveal too much of himself to any casual observer. She had imagined that whereas he might be an excellent friend it would not be easy for him to make friends in a short space of time. He was too intelligent and too experienced to give too much of himself too soon. She did not think him a man of impulse. Perhaps his weariness, his struggle with some personal anxiety, had caused him to relax his guard, or else she had struck the right note with her impersonal friendliness. For he had been at ease with her, accepting her without question, encouraging her to air her views, challenging her like an old and familiar friend, and she felt that whatever he had unconsciously sought in her, she had not failed him.

Had it been impulse or instinct that led him to drive her home, to accept her invitation of coffee? It did not really matter. She had sensed that he was weary and troubled and she had offered him practical comfort. She had offered him relaxation, a brief forgetfulness of his problems, light conversation and a meal — and the hand of friendship that would involve him in nothing more unless he wished it.

But how could he have known that she would not attach undue importance to that brief encounter, would not recount the incident to her friends with much embroidering, would not create a hum of gossip he could scarcely welcome as a man about to be married? He knew very little about her — he had not even known her name. She could only suppose, with a faintly wry twist to her mouth, that her detachment, her coolness and matter of fact approach was more in evidence than she realised.

Of course, it might merely be a case of a man at the end of his tether after a week of great strain and desperately in need of human contact — preferably with someone impersonal, someone he scarcely knew, someone who demanded no more of him than a little light conversation. It seemed to Honor that something had disturbed him very much, kicked away the solid foundations beneath his feet — and she could only hope that he had left her that evening with the feeling that he was gradually beginning to get his bearings.

It was difficult to believe that he was planning to marry in the near future. It had been something of a shock — but not in the way that Joy might imagine. It was just that he did not seem the happy prospective bridegroom that one would expect. On the verge of marriage — yet so unhappy, so bitter, so weighed down with despair that he might be a man who had suffered a great loss or disappointment.

Perhaps he didn't wish to be married, after all — and was too much a man of integrity to break his engagement at this late date. Perhaps he was being forced into marriage with a woman he did not love for some reason he could not escape. Perhaps he was persuading into marriage a woman he knew did not love him.

But Honor could not reconcile any of these suppositions with the man she admittedly did not know very well and yet oddly felt she had always known. He was not a man to do anything against his will — and neither would he shrink from the unpleasantness of admitting a change of heart at the last moment, even though it might mean hurting the woman who loved him. No one could really imagine a man of his personality and character being forced into a marriage he did not welcome for any reason. Neither would he marry a woman unless he was sure of her love and confident of their happiness in marriage. He was proud and sensitive, an intelligent, responsible, mature man who knew where he was going and what he wanted in life. Not a man to make foolish mistakes, to take impetuous steps, to allow his heart to rule his head no matter how deeply in love he might be.

Honor reminded herself that she had no reason to believe that his anxiety had anything to do with his engagement or approaching marriage. He was going to London to straighten things out, she imagined — and presumably he would spend some time with his fiancee, but she had no reason to suspect that the two events were connected in any way.

And, in any case, it was really none of her business, she added, rebuking herself. Like Joy, she was probably making a big thing out of very little. If he had wanted her to know anything about his personal affairs he would have told her and it was really rather presumptuous of her to lie in her bath and worry about him.

For she was worried. She felt that she

had not done enough, that she should have encouraged him to unburden his anxiety, that she should not have let him leave at that particular moment when she had sensed that he was on the verge of speaking of personal matters. Why else had he told her about his house in Oaklands Drive and spoken of its lack of furnishings and comfort if he hadn't expected her to comment on his plans to marry very soon? He must know that it was fairly common knowledge at St. Antony's — and Honor would have known about it if she had bothered to listen to the Common Room chatter.

She wondered if it would have made any difference to her attitude to him if she had known. She would possibly not have felt so much at ease with him, certainly would not have invited him in for coffee — and thus would have missed a pleasant evening with a man who was not easy to know but very easy to like.

Suddenly Honor sat bolt upright in

her bath. He had asked her to have dinner with him one evening! Surely he could not have been serious — men who were engaged to be married did not take other women out to dinner unless they were asking for trouble. However innocent their friendship might be, the gossip-mongers would distort it — and in a small community like St. Antony's no one could hope to escape the eyes and ears of the curious and talkative. He must have spoken lightly, the kind of thing that people did say without any intention of carrying it out — after all, there had been nothing definite about the invitation and, she remembered, she had certainly not said that she would go out with him.

Realising the coldness of the water, she knew that she had been dawdling over her bath, preoccupied with the thought of Calder Savage and, determined not to think about him again that night, she stepped out of the bath and wrapped her slim body in a huge bathtowel.

Joy banged on the bathroom door. "Are you all right in there, ducky?"

"Just coming!"

"Do you want a sandwich? The milk is on for the nightcap."

"No thanks. I'll be out in a minute."

Within a very few minutes, in pyjamas and dressing-gown, she was curled up on her bed with a steaming mug of hot milk cradled in both hands, watching Joy as she unpinned her long, dark hair and began to brush it with even, methodical strokes of the brush.

"Did you have a nice time today?" she asked, a little contritely, having completely forgotten that Joy had spent the afternoon with her relatives until this moment.

Joy shrugged. "So-so. Mike's down from Oxford and I find him rather irritating. He insisted that we play tennis which just isn't my game, and then spent most of the time pointing out my faults."

"Poor old girl, you never did take to criticism kindly," Honor teased.

"I could bear that if he didn't bore me to death with car mechanics when he isn't being athletic and hearty. I like cars but I'm a passenger by nature and common sense. I don't want to know how they work — and I don't want to learn to drive."

"Sensible girl! You're so easily distracted that you'd be off the road in five minutes — still staring at the attractive man who'd caught your eye!"

"Quite probably," Joy agreed complacently, quite inured to Honor's teasing remarks.

"Mike brought you home, obviously."

"I couldn't dissuade him and, frankly, I didn't try very hard. If it's a choice between the train journey and Mike's conversation I'll take the lesser of the two evils any time. I suppose I was a bit offhand with him, actually. I was so astonished to see you hand in hand with the SSO that I scarcely thanked him for bringing me home and never thought of asking him in for some coffee."

"Which proves that he's possibly the only man of eligible age and suitability who doesn't interest you in the least," Honor said quickly in order to distract Joy from renewing the subject of Calder Savage.

"Interest me? Mike! You must be joking. For one thing, I've known him all my life and I'm just about fed up with his patronising attitude. For another, he hasn't even got any looks to recommend him."

"Oh, that isn't important! Anyway, he has a very pleasant face and really attractive eyes. I rather like Mike . . . and sometimes I think that the boy next door, so to speak, might be the best person for you to settle down with, in the long run."

Joy turned to stare at her, speechless. But only for a moment. "Thanks very much! I'd rather devote my life to nursing and end up as Matron than marry 'good old Mike, the life and soul of the party'. I told you — he patronises me! He always has done since we were children. You should listen to him giving me good advice on how to run my life and my affairs!"

"Perhaps it is good advice," Honor said, smiling.

"You should have heard him all the way home . . . " Joy began indignantly and Honor settled down to listen with half an ear and to murmur soothingly at intervals.

She sometimes suspected that Joy's resentment and annoyance sprang from Mike's attitude which, while being far from loverlike, was certainly rather proprietorial. And Honor knew that, provided Joy was not swept into marriage on an impulse in the meantime, she would probably marry Mike Ferris one day and be ideally happy.

★ ★ ★

Honor paused in her musings as she became aware of a car cruising slowly down the road beside her. She hesitated and frowned slightly. She could not see the driver clearly but she was sure that she recognised the car.

The driver braked and moved across to the nearside window — it was Calder Savage.

"Good morning!" he called. "You're out bright and early."

Honor went over to the car. "Good morning," she returned lightly. "I thought you were in London."

He gave a brief shrug of his broad shoulders. "I felt homesick."

She smiled. "Are you going to St. Antony's?"

"No. It's a nice morning and I felt like a drive." He smiled up at her, and she was surprised at the surge of happiness that ran through her at the sight of that quick smile. "Are you on your way home?" he asked.

"Yes."

He must have realised the significance of the small hat she wore. "You've been to church," he guessed.

Honor nodded. "I like to go," she said, a little shyly. "My father was a minister, you see, and although he never insisted that I should attend the services it would have seemed disloyal to stay away. It still would."

"Do you have to rush back to the flat? Will you have some coffee with me? I think I noticed a coffee bar a little way down the road — and it seemed to be open."

"Mike's Bar," she said a little doubtfully. "I don't think it's quite your type of place, Mr. Savage."

"I only insist on good coffee — the decor won't bother me," he assured her.

"Their coffee is excellent, but it's very popular with the local teenagers."

"Am I so old and decrepit that I'll be totally out of place?"

"No, of course not. But if you'd like some coffee, I'll make it in a moment," she offered tentatively.

He opened the car door. "I don't mean to make a habit of encroaching on your hospitality, you know," he warned her lightly. "But your coffee is too much of a temptation to pass up, I'm afraid."

Honor still hesitated and he showed his surprise.

"What is it?" he asked quietly.

"Joy," she said. "She isn't on duty until two o'clock."

"I see." He patted the car seat. "Then it's Mike's Bar despite the teenagers."

Honor climbed in beside him and he drove down the High Street at a leisurely pace.

"Not that I have any aversion to meeting your friend," he added reassuringly. "But not this particular morning. I hope you understand."

Honor did understand. Despite his seeming light-heartedness, his ready smiles and banter, she sensed that he was making an effort. She wondered what had gone wrong with his week-end that he had returned to Camhurst so abruptly. A tiff with his fiancée — or further unpleasant developments in the matter which had troubled him all the previous week? There was tension behind his smile, a look of strain in his eyes that was even greater than that at their last encounter, a tautness in the hands that gripped the steering wheel and an unhappiness so intense in his whole being that she sensed it swiftly and knew again that odd, tender stirring of compassion.

★ ★ ★

Honor watched Calder Savage as he waited for the ordered coffees. He had settled her in a corner seat by the window in the small, contemporary coffee bar that was comparatively quiet at this particular time on a Sunday morning.

He was an attractive man, she conceded. He was, in fact, remarkably handsome but Honor did not judge any man by looks alone and when she thought of him as attractive it was his personality rather than appearance that motivated the description. In retrospect, it was extremely odd that they should have slipped so easily into friendship on the strength of a few trivial remarks, the short journey to her flat in his car and the impulsive invitation she had offered on their arrival. He was some years older, much more experienced and worldly-wise and engaged to be married — and she could not disregard the fact that Matron would certainly frown on any hint of friendship between a senior surgeon and a comparatively junior member of her nursing staff.

Honor was vaguely troubled by the feeling that she should not have taken matters any further than accepting the offered lift and thanking him politely when he dropped her at the corner of her road. He had accepted her invitation to coffee with flattering promptness — but she could not imagine why. He could have no real interest in creating a friendship with a nurse from St. Antony's. For one thing, it was obvious that he would not welcome any hint of gossip when he was on the verge of marrying another woman — for another, they were worlds apart. She was very much his junior, both in years and professionally. She was no great conversationalist, no beauty, no social success — and yet, they had undeniably slipped with ease into a quiet, pleasant and undemanding friendship.

Unaccountably, he had been much in her thoughts over the week-end. She had been quite unable to forget the haunting pain and sadness in his eyes, the bitterness that seemed to betray itself in occasional remarks, the conviction that simply by being herself and by accepting him as he was she had supplied some need of which he might not even have been fully conscious.

He came to her, interrupting her thoughts, carrying the brimming cups with great care and smiling at her across the room. His smile held all the intimate warmth of friendship that was almost tinged with affection, and there was a boyish kind of camaraderie in the manner with which he successfully placed the cups on the table — cups so full yet miraculously not overflowing into the saucers.

"How's that for steady hands?" he demanded with a triumphant grin.

"It would be surprising if they weren't steady considering the work that you do," she retorted with a faint smile.

He slipped into the seat beside her. The high back of the padded seat provided them with privacy and only the raucous strains of the busy juke-box prevented them from feeling that they were in a world of their own.

"Yes, I suppose so," he agreed.

"Do you want to talk shop?"

"Not particularly — it's nice to forget the demands of the profession for a few hours."

She nodded. "It is demanding, I know. But you love it really, don't you?"

"I'm not particularly good at anything I don't enjoy," he countered. "Surgery appealed to me from the early days. I enjoy it and I've worked hard to be a good surgeon."

"Do you ever regret it?"

He did not reply for a moment. Then he said slowly: "Only inasmuch that it hasn't left me very much time for my personal life."

"I think most doctors and surgeons feel that," Honor said quietly. "Perhaps that's why they often marry someone in the same profession, someone who understands its demands and will make allowances for them."

"Quite possibly," he agreed, almost curtly. "But we agreed not to talk shop," he reminded her with a smile that was intended to take the sting from his curt retort.

"So we did — but one always seems to revert to it," she said ruefully. "I'm sorry."

"I'm sorry I snapped," he said generously. "I'm just a little edgy."

"Bad week-end?" she asked gently.

"Not too good — a complete waste of time, as a matter of fact I went to see my fiancée . . . "

"She's a nurse, too, isn't she?" Honor did not mean to break into his words but she was so oddly relieved that he had mentioned his fiancée that she spoke impulsively — and a little too quickly. Joy's remarks had rankled slightly — and she did not want to think that he might be deliberately refraining from mentioning the fact that he was engaged to be married. He did not seem the type of man to show interest in another woman when he was pledged to one, and although she had argued that the subject of his fiancée had not arisen when they were together on Friday evening there had been the faint doubt in her mind that perhaps he should have brought her into the conversation in some way. After all, his interest might have appeared very marked to a different type of girl, someone like Joy, for instance — and the average man would take some pains to avoid that interest being misinterpreted.

Calder glanced at her quickly, his hand stilled in the act of stirring his coffee. "So it is common knowledge," he said harshly, almost angrily.

Honor was at a loss to understand that swift and obvious annoyance. He must know that he had been the subject of much discussion and speculation during the few weeks that he had been at St. Antony's. "Why, yes. You haven't forgotten that hospitals are hot-beds of gossip, surely?" she returned lightly. "Everyone wants to know all there is to know about a new arrival, especially a new SSO. I imagine everyone knows that you're engaged to a Sister at a London hospital and that you're getting married very soon." She smiled at him gently. "Isn't that why you bought a house instead of renting a bachelor flat?"

"It is and now I shall be putting it on the market again," he said flatly.

Honor looked at him quickly. "The wedding is off?"

"Very much so, the lady has changed

98

her mind." Bitterness and anger touched his voice.

Honor caught her breath. So that was the reason for his unhappiness and despair — and the unexpectedly abrupt return from London. Obviously he had gone to see the girl to try to patch things up, without success.

"I'm sorry," she said gently.

He took a cigarette from the packet he had thrown on to the table. Belatedly, he remembered to offer the packet to Honor and she shook her head.

"I really am sorry," she told him quietly.

"Why should you be? We scarcely know each other!"

Honor coloured faintly. His retort was a definite snub — and she was hurt. But it was in such violent contrast with his previous kindly manner that she decided that he had spoken harshly out of pain and abrupt regret for having confided in her.

"Well, it's very hard for you — just

now," she said with compassion tinging her voice. "You've worked so hard. And now — well, this job must have been a feather in your cap and I expect you wanted to share your success and elation with someone who would appreciate your efforts to get where you wanted."

"Yes, it's been hard work — and it was an unexpected stroke of luck to get this post," he admitted slowly.

"Not entirely luck, surely? Not many men have your qualifications at such an early age."

He smiled faintly. "I am thirty-five, you know — not so very young."

"You'll be a consultant surgeon before you're forty," she said confidently.

He turned his cigarette between his fingers. "I wonder. It was my ambition, but now I'm not so sure that it's so important. I've achieved material success — but my personal affairs have had to foot the bill." Abruptly, he stubbed his cigarette. "Heaven knows why I'm inflicting my personal problems on you. They're scarcely a cheerful topic of conversation for a bright Sunday morning." There was a faint edge to his voice. "I suppose your youthful philosophy includes a practical approach to a broken engagement — advising me to take the view that there are other pebbles on the beach, for instance?"

"That was an unkind sneer," she said quietly.

Their eyes met. Grey eyes holding a candid reproach looked into dark eyes that held pain and bewilderment and a plea for understanding in their depths.

"Yes, I'm sorry," he said with sincerity. He ran a hand over his hair. "I'm not really fit company for anyone this morning, Honor, and it isn't fair that you should bear the brunt of my ill humour."

The absent use of her first name brought a sudden warmth to her heart. She would not have been surprised to learn that he had forgotten her name, certainly it was pleasant to realise that he not only knew it but had not hesitated to use it.

She said impulsively: "I want to help even if it's only by being with you at a time when you don't want to be alone."

He covered her hand with his own. "Thank you. You do help. I'm feeling ridiculously sorry for myself — and you're so sensible and reassuring that I'm beginning to wonder why I'm making so much fuss about something that happens to many men. It isn't the end of the world, after all."

For the first time in her life, Honor was not sure that she wanted a man to think of her as sensible and prosaic and unemotional. His words made her feel like a practical spinster who, while never having experienced the shattering ups and downs of emotional stress, had acquired a logical and penetrating knowledge of life in her rôle as spectator.

"My feelings aren't involved," she

admitted frankly. "It would be easy for me to spout a great many platitudes — but you wouldn't believe any of them just now and it would only irritate you intensely. I expect it does seem the end of everything you've worked for and dreamed about for years, the end of your world for the time being. It would be the end of my world if it happened to me — and philosophy isn't much help. One knows what one should do and say and feel in the circumstances — but that's just theory and it seems ridiculous when one is really faced with a personal problem that overturns one's whole life."

There was something in her tone that caused him to half-turn in his seat and study her face with narrowed eyes. "Has it happened to you, Honor? You're very young."

"I've never been in love," she told him frankly.

"Wise girl!" he returned bitterly. "Take my advice and stay clear of it . . . unless you can be really sure that it isn't going to bring you a lot of heartache and disappointment."

She smiled. "Can one ever be really sure?"

"No, darn it! I thought I was sure, but people are so unreliable!"

"What went wrong?" she asked quietly. She put the question on an impulse and immediately regretted it. "Oh, I'm sorry — I don't mean to be inquisitive and I'm sure you don't really want to talk about it."

"Oddly enough, I don't mind in the least," he told her with a faint smile. "I don't resent your questions . . . I should leap down your throat if I did, believe me!"

He told her, concisely and without emotion, of Heather's letter, the unsatisfactory telephone call, his decision to travel to London at the week-end to straighten things out and the uncompromising attitude that Heather had taken without going into unnecessary details — and the quiet detachment of the recital conveyed in full measure the pain and disappointment and bewilderment he had suffered.

Honor listened in silence. She could not condemn the unknown Heather but she did feel that the woman had been rather foolish and thoughtless to allow matters to drift needlessly for so long. It must have been obvious that she had to hurt the man who loved her. Postponement had increased rather than lessened the hurt and now he had to face the humiliation that everyone in Camhurst would have known that it ever existed, that almost every member of St. Antony's staff knew that he was expecting to be married within a matter of weeks, that his fiancee was a nurse and that he had bought a house solely to provide a home for his bride. Gossip and speculation would run rife when it became obvious that he was not going to be married, after all.

"You'd been engaged for a long time?" she asked at length when he stopped speaking.

Calder nodded. "Almost eight years."

"It seems strange that she should suddenly change her mind after such a long time."

He shrugged. "She claims that it was too long to wait, and I expect she's right. It hasn't been easy for either of us at times. My fault, I admit. Heather wanted us to marry years ago but I was determined to make the grade before taking on the responsibility of a wife. It doesn't pay to be too sure of people. I've never doubted the strength and lasting powers of Heather's feeling for me and perhaps I should have done. Perhaps I should have had enough perception to realise that she was getting bored and restless — I suppose it isn't really so surprising. Not many women would have had Heather's patience and understanding; it isn't really her fault that it eventually wore thin."

"Don't you think this might be just a passing thing? When one has waited years for something and grown used to waiting it can't be easy to adjust to the sudden realisation that it's actually within your grasp. Perhaps this is just a temporary panic, a feeling that you might both have made a mistake — a fear that you might be suited enough for an engagement but might make a dreadful hash of marriage. It isn't impossible, is it?"

"No, I agree. But would you really advise me to think along those lines? I would only be storing up more disappointment, more heartache if the months went by and Heather didn't realise that she still wanted to marry me. No, I must accept that it's ended . . . make a new life without her."

"And possibly you'll find that you don't want her when she does realise her mistake!" Honor interjected.

"That's the chance one has to take! I should be very sorry if that turned out to be the case — sorry for Heather — but she has broken our engagement and she must take the consequences if she's made a mistake," he said quickly. "I don't intend to spend the rest of my life loving a woman — who threw me over a few weeks before we were supposed to be married. I'm not the forgiving kind. I wouldn't give any woman a second chance to hurt and humiliate me, and I shall take steps to ensure that I never meet Heather again in any circumstances!" He smiled with faint bitterness. "You're a romantic despite your practical philosophies, my dear, but I can assure you that there isn't the least likelihood that Heather will regret breaking our engagement and I certainly won't go into a decline because of one disappointment. 'Men have died from time to time . . . but not for love'," he reminded her, a little grimly.

"I suppose I am romantic, but I should like you to be happy," Honor said quietly.

He raised an eyebrow. "What is happiness? One can always work."

She studied him with some compassion, although she agreed that his love and dedication for his work would no doubt go a long way to ease his sense of loss and disappointment. She also realised that he was the kind of man who would slip easily into confirmed bachelorhood with scarcely a thought, in time, for what he might be missing in life. Honor had never considered marriage for herself — possibly because it had never occurred to her that any man could wish to marry her — but she was enough of a romantic and an idealist to believe that marriage could bring the ultimate happiness to almost every individual, provided that love and understanding and tolerance formed its basis. She sensed that Calder Savage had all the necessary qualities that went into the making of a good husband, and it seemed a waste that he should be denied the chance to prove it.

"And perhaps you'll meet someone else who won't let you down one day," she said a little shyly.

He made no reply and she understood his reluctance to even think along those lines at this particular time. He was much too deeply hurt, much too grieved by the loss of the woman he loved to find any consolation in the thought of a possible replacement for her in time. At the moment, understandably, he must feel that it was impossible for him to care for any other woman as he cared for his ex-fiancée. Honor hoped with all her heart that the unknown Heather would realise the emptiness of her life without the man she had expected to marry for so many years, and that Calder would not have ceased to love her by the time she came to her senses. Eight years was a very long time. They must know each other intimately and feel that their lives were irrevocably intertwined. It scarcely seemed possible that they could simply part so abruptly and make new lives for themselves with ease and without regret. It was very obvious that it would not be easy for Calder — and that he regretted Heather's change of heart intensely. Perhaps it would be equally difficult for her and perhaps she would soon begin to regret. Honor's kind heart was touched by her new friend's pain and she wished there was some way she could take to help him regain the happiness he had known. But she could not interfere in his personal affairs; she could only be at hand when, and if, he wanted a friend for company and consolation and comfort.

4

CALDER abruptly realised that he was humming as he drove to the hospital, and was faintly surprised to discover that he was in a reasonably cheerful frame of mind. Certainly the black pall of depression had lifted since the previous day. Whether this was due to the natural resilience of the human heart or whether he could thank the undemanding Honor Portland for this strange phenomenon, he was not quite certain.

It was not until he was on his way home in the early evening that he thought over the hours he had spent with her with grateful appreciation of her comforting and reassuring talent for dropping the subject of Heather and turning his thoughts to more agreeable things. He still thought it odd that he had been able to talk to her of his feeling with so little reserve, but it had eased the heartache and humiliation and brought him to the point where he could accept the inevitable and admit that though he might never know the happiness he had hoped for with Heather it was possible that he could find a measure of contentment in a life without her.

Despite the swift, proud retort he had made to Honor's tentative suggestion that Heather might regret the break with him, he had gained a degree of comfort from the thought. There had been a great deal of sense in the explanation that the young girl had offered for Heather's abrupt and seemingly inexplicable change of heart. It might very well contain an element of truth.

After all, he had forced himself to be content with the self-imposed postponement of their marriage. It had been exceedingly difficult in the early days but had gradually become easier as the months and then the years slowly consumed their youth and their impatience. He had eventually slipped into thinking of their marriage only at long intervals or when Heather hesitantly brought up the subject. It was an event that would take place at some distant date, and the less one thought about the fulfilment and the promised happiness of that marriage the easier it was to reconcile oneself to the long wait. In all honesty, he could not claim that his first reaction to his acceptance as the Senior Surgical Officer at St. Antony's had been the thought that now he and Heather could be married. He had known elation, relief, a sense of achievement, a certain satisfaction with the fruits of his labours — but the realisation that he could now claim the happiness he had denied himself and Heather for so long had been a secondary and, frankly, less important satisfaction. He could scarcely blame Heather if her feelings had coincided with his.

But his love had not died during

those long years. It was a stable, assured and natural belief that Heather was the only woman he would ever want to marry, the only woman of any importance in his life, the only woman who could give him the happiness he desired.

His well-kept, strong hands tightened on the wheel as a sudden thought stirred in his mind. Was it possible that he had continued to love Heather only because he had never been attracted to any other woman, never allowed himself the time or the inclination to feel an interest in any other woman? Would his love have survived if there had been other women in his life as there had undeniably been other men in Heather's life, albeit relatively unimportant to her? Had he immersed himself in his work to such an extent that he had deliberately chosen, if unconsciously, to maintain an idealistic kind of love for a woman who made few demands on him? For Heather had been patient, understanding, loyal, more so than he would have expected of any woman. Maybe because in her heart of hearts she did not really love him very deeply and therefore was not as impatient for marriage as she should have been. Maybe because she had long since accepted the truth to which he had been blind all these years — that he was not deeply enough in love to really wish for marriage while his work absorbed his emotions and energies, his hopes and his dreams, his time and his interest. If she had lost heart and ceased to believe in the promise of a shared future she might yet have cared sufficiently for him and little enough for the thought of marriage to any man to drift, leaving things as they were, content with the little he gave her.

But he would have married her. He had bought a house, talked of his wedding plans, made certain preparations for their marriage.

Now he had to face the possibility that he would have entered into marriage because the idea of it had become a habit, not because he truly loved and desired Heather for his wife but because he was bound by a pledge made almost eight year's before and felt that the bonds that held him to Heather were not lightly broken; because a man in his position needed a wife and it would be easy to drift into marriage with Heather, even though he might not really be in love with her or any woman.

He could not be sure if any of these thoughts had their basis in truth. But he did realise that it would have been wrong to marry Heather when his heart had not really leapt at the thought of doing so when he learned of his new post at St. Antony's. Unpalatable though it was, he also had to admit that Heather's claim that she had never been of primary importance and consideration in his life was undeniably true. His work, his ambitions, his ideals had always come before Heather, even when he had believed himself to be most ardently in love. The original heady emotion that Heather inspired in him had been replaced by a more stable, less intoxicating feeling, which made him wonder now if the first had been infatuation born of physical attraction and if the latter had been a deep affection and gratitude that he had mistaken for a mature and lasting love.

There was no answer to the problem at this stage. Only time would prove the point and straighten out the confusion of his thoughts and emotions. Either he would continue to mourn the loss of Heather and fail to find any consolation in life for the happiness he had been denied — or he would find it comparatively easy to fill the void that her going had created and eventually discover that his thoughts were turning to the contemplation of marriage with someone else.

He would never know the truth if he followed that first impulse to steer clear of feminine charms in the future. He could never be a libertine but there was no reason why he should not seek out the company of other women and give himself the chance to discover if he was really capable of love, if he had given his heart to Heather for all time or if it was frankly and wholly impossible for any woman to be of primary importance in his life!

Without conceit, he knew that he was attractive to women, and there were women in plenty in the world for whom he could surely know a natural attraction if he allowed himself the time and the inclination.

On this last thought, with a faint smile touching the corner of his mouth, he turned into the gates of St. Antony's and returned the greeting of the porter at his lodge.

He was not operating that morning and he had a certain amount of paper work to deal with. The morning passed swiftly, broken by ward rounds, visits from the Secretary of the Hospital Committee and Sir Justin Lee, the consultant surgeon, telephone calls and various other interruptions. He was much too busy to think about his personal affairs and his cheerfulness increased as the day wore on and work progressed smoothly.

It was not until he joined the RSO for coffee in the common room that he discovered that the hospital was seething with rumours about him and Honor Portland. He might not have known then except for the sudden silence that fell on the hum of conversation as he entered the room with Harper. It momentarily struck him as odd but he was interested in the case he was discussing with Harper and he would have thought no more of it if he had not noticed the gleam of amused speculation in Sir Justin's glance and a betraying discomfiture in the swift exit of a houseman who had been standing by his side.

"Someone taking my name in vain?" he asked lightly as Harper, sensing a certain restraint in the atmosphere, fell silent. The two men crossed the room to join Sir Justin who turned to pour coffee for himself and them.

"I hear that you've caused something of a stir among our nurses, Savage," he said dryly, a humorous twinkle in his eyes.

Calder frowned. "Sir . . . ?"

Sir Justin handed him a cup of coffee. He was not a man to stand on ceremony and he liked the easy informality of the common room. He also liked what he had seen of the new SSO and being both blunt and sympathetic he did not hesitate to acquaint him with the rumours that had been sweeping the hospital.

"Come, come, man — no need to play the innocent," he retorted with a chuckle. "The whole hospital is agog — and I must say I thought you had too much sense than to speak more than twice to the same nurse for fear of finding yourself accused of unsavoury intentions!"

Bewilderment mingled with anger and it was with an effort that he controlled the spasm of temper that shook him. "You will have to be a little more explicit, Sir Justin," he said rather coldly. "I'm afraid I have no idea of your meaning."

Sir Justin grinned. "I'm told that you've been playing fast and loose with a Staff Nurse. Can't say I blame you — some of them are darned attractive, but it really doesn't pay to mix business with pleasure — not in our profession, anyway!"

Calder's mouth tightened grimly. "Now I think I understand you, Sir Justin. But you have mistaken the matter, you know. I have enough experience of hospital life to avoid creating food for gossip, and I can assure you that I scarcely know the nurse in question."

"No need to tell me any such thing, Savage. I think I know you well enough to be aware that the rumours are founded on a perfectly innocent exchange. But you won't stop people gossiping — and it's all very harmless provided one doesn't take it too seriously. Don't get your back up, man, that's the surest way to make people think there must be something behind the talk. If you'll forgive the impertinence of offering you advice, might I suggest that you take pains to kill the rumours by avoiding the nurse in question as much as possible?"

"I appreciate your concern for my reputation and for the good name of the nursing staff, Sir Justin — but your advice is both impertinent and presumptuous — if you'll forgive my frankness. My personal affairs are my concern and I can scarcely think that they are likely to cause yourself, the Hospital Committee or Matron any anxiety, and I can assure you that any rumours that have reached your ears are the figment of an overworked imagination!"

"Might well be," Sir Justin agreed amicably, unruffled by the suppressed anger and resentment of the younger man's tone. "Just thought a word of warning in your ear might avert any unpleasantness. No one likes gossip, of course . . . "

"And everyone indulges in it!" Calder returned bitingly. He set down his untouched coffee, told Harper that he would see him later and left with the briefest of nods for Sir Justin.

Calder went to his office and sat down to the papers that still remained on his desk. He forced himself to concentrate on the work, thrusting the anger and dismay from his thoughts for the time being.

But when the papers were dealt with and pushed to one side, he sat back in his chair, frowning, recalling the conversation he had exchanged with Sir Justin. It was obvious that Honor Portland was the name that had been linked with his, she was the only Staff Nurse who might have been seen in his company and he had been too circumspect to exchange more than brief, formal pleasantries with any other nurse who came in his way.

The gossip in itself did not trouble him. It was not so surprising if they had been seen together and as a newcomer to St. Antony's he was obviously eligible food for gossip. But he was perceptive enough to realise that Sir Justin had not told him the whole — that there must be more to the gossip than the fact that he and Honor had been seen together by chance. Sir Justin evidently half-believed the rumours and the glint in his eyes indicated that he was both amused and a little astonished to discover that a fellow surgeon had been indiscreet. Calder had a clear conscience — and he could almost be amused himself by the spate of talk that had arisen from such a trivial affair, but for one thing.

For it seemed to Calder unmistakably certain that Honor had gossiped to her friends about her relationship with him, and embroidered on something that had never been anything more than innocent and incidental — and not only because there had scarcely been time for it to develop beyond mere friendliness and a liking for each other's company.

He was disappointed and dismayed. She had not seemed the type of girl to flaunt her conquests — or to attach enough importance to their brief relationship to call him a conquest — which he certainly was not! But it merely proved how little he really did know about women — and he was disheartened. He had hoped that in Honor Portland he had found a rare friend; rare because such a friendship as he visualised seldom existed between the sexes. He was angry at the thought that she had taken the first opportunity to spread it about St. Antony's that the new SSO was interested in her. No doubt his feeling of warm friendliness, which he had never tried to disguise, had been misinterpreted — and to Honor it was something to enhance her importance in the eyes of her colleagues, something to broadcast and to gloat over, some small triumph over the fellow nurses who had so blatantly tried to attract his notice and failed.

He remembered now that she had accosted him, had spoken with easy familiarity and friendliness, had made it easy and natural for him to offer her a lift — and then had taken matters further by inviting him to the flat for coffee. At the time he had been warmed by her friendliness and evident understanding and perception. Now he realised that he had been as gullible as any raw youth and had blindly walked into a prepared snare. Certainly her behaviour was not that of a circumspect and cautious nurse who knew better than to strike up a friendship with a senior member of the staff. His lip curled as he remembered that she had warned him that people would talk if they were seen together — and he had dismissed the warning as nonsense. He had entirely been led astray by the seeming candour of those grey eyes, by the deceptive sweetness of her smile, by the unexpected method of her approach; an approach which, he realised now, had been as blatant as any of the others he had rebuffed. He reminded himself that he had been weary and dispirited and ready to be grateful for a kind and friendly word from anyone — but that was really no excuse for his lack of perception.

There was an obvious remedy, of course — and he had not needed Sir Justin's injunction to take steps to suppress the gossip. He had to protect his reputation and in doing so he would also protect the reputation of the girl who had apparently chosen to cast it under suspicion. Had he been strongly attracted to Honor Portland there would still have been no alternative for him to impress upon every member of St. Antony's staff that she was no more than a cog in the wheel as far as he was concerned.

It was fortunate that he felt no such attraction — and the course he would take was made easier by the knowledge that her unexpected and disappointing behaviour had nipped in the bud any feeling of affection which might have flowered if their friendship had been allowed to develop.

5

HONOR felt a stir of anticipation as she heard Calder's voice in the changing-room. She bent over the instrument trolley and went on with her work but her heart began to beat a little faster at the thought that within a few moments they would meet. She wondered how he would greet her, discreetly, of course, and with the pleasant courtesy she had come to expect from him before that spell of irritability and bad temper. But surely there would be a certain warmth in his eyes for her recognition alone, surely there would be a faint recollection of the hours they had spent together on the previous day in his smile and voice. It had been a happy day and he had seemed more relaxed, more cheerful once they left Mike's Bar and set off in his car for the countryside.

They had lunched at a small pub and then walked beside the river in perfect harmony, content to talk little but each aware of that companionable and warming quality in their silence. Reluctantly she had reminded him that both must work on the following day and there were certain things she must do that evening, and he had driven her back to the flat, thanked her for her company, apologised again for inflicting his problems on her, assured her that she had helped a great deal and left her on the promise that there would be many more days spent in each other's company.

Honor was too wise to read more into his promise than he intended, and it was too early in their friendship to imagine that he thought of her as anything but a friend. She was not so foolish as to fancy herself in love with him on the strength of a few hours in his company, but she liked him immensely and hoped that both would gain a great deal from their friendship. At the moment, she could in all sincerity hope that his personal affairs would resolve themselves satisfactorily and that he would eventually find his happiness with the unknown Heather. Perhaps in time, as their friendship developed and affection grew between them, she might find herself hoping that Heather would remain unattainable and that Calder would get over his disappointment and find consolation in her arms. But Honor was determined not to think along those lines. She only knew that no man had ever stirred her so deeply as Calder Savage. Whether or not that stirring was the beginning of love for him was a question that only time would answer.

She was in Theatre when he entered, ready for operating in gown, cap and mask. She knew he could not see her welcoming smile but her eyes would convey it to him — and she turned towards him. Their eyes met — and then he deliberately turned away and spoke to the anaesthetist. An icy shock touched Honor's heart for his gaze had been cold and forbidding, and she did not doubt that his slow, calculated movement had been a deliberate and inexplicable snub.

As the afternoon wore on, Honor knew she had not been mistaken. He completely ignored her except when it was necessary for them to speak — which was seldom. He was so remote, so hostile that Honor wondered if he regretted the friendly intimacy of the previous day and the impulse which had led him to seek her out and confide in her as he had done. She had not expected him to be more than pleasant and quietly friendly, of course, but it hurt to realise that he was deliberately behaving as though they had never spoken outside Theatre, never reached so rapidly the terms of mutual liking and easy intimacy.

She could not even deceive herself that he was falling over backwards in an attempt to protect them both from staff gossip, for he set himself to be pleasant and friendly and even-tempered as though to make amends for the churlishness of the previous week and to retrieve the former liking and respect of Theatre staff. It was only to Honor that he was curt and unfriendly, but she fully realised that he did not know how pointed his manner towards her was in contrast with his manner towards the others. She did not think the others would notice anything amiss — and that was some small consolation.

But she was hurt, much more than she cared to admit. She knew that those who talked too freely on impulse into a receptive ear very soon wished they had not said quite so much — and, conscious of embarrassment and a sense of having invited an intrusion into their privacy, chose to avoid the person who had been the recipient of regretted confidences. That was a very common revulsion of feeling — but she had not expected it from Calder Savage and she was disappointed and a little annoyed.

It was not imagination. Calder was snubbing her — and she was not the only one to notice it despite her hope to the contrary. At the end of the afternoon, when the SSO and his assistant and the anaesthetist had left Theatre, Sister eyed Honor curiously and then crossed the room to her and asked bluntly if she had annoyed Mr. Savage in any way.

Honor stiffened at the question. Faint colour stole into her cheeks. "I don't think so, Sister," she said coolly, disturbed and resentful that Calder's odd attitude should have attracted Sister's attention.

"Hm! Well, his mood is much easier for everyone this week, but it seemed to me that he had very little courtesy or friendliness for you, Nurse."

"I didn't notice anything in his manner, Sister," Honor replied mendaciously, embarrassed, humiliated and very angry.

"Oh, well, perhaps I imagined it. But it isn't unusual for a surgeon to take a violent and unreasonable dislike to a member of Theatre staff — I've met that kind of thing before. I hope Mr. Savage doesn't expect me to request the transfer of one of my best nurses merely to satisfy some foolish whim of his." She smiled and patted Honor's shoulder. "Very well, Nurse . . . you may carry on with your work now."

Honor's heart welled within her as she turned away. It was not in character for Sister to be so unbending . . . and that sympathetic smile and gentle pat had been almost more than Honor could bear. Life in Theatre would be intolerable if Calder meant to continue the strange, baffling hostility he had abruptly introduced — for she would soon be the pivot of everyone's sympathy and curiosity.

She leaned wearily against the wall, unseen by the two juniors who were ostensibly sterilising the instruments while they gleefully discussed the one excitement in an uneventful day.

At first, Honor took no notice of

their chatter; then gradually, what they were saying penetrated her misery.

" . . . I must say I wouldn't have been in Portland's shoes today for anything! I wonder what she's done to upset him."

"Probably went off with him for the week-end and then declined to keep her part of the bargain at the last minute," came the swift, mischievous retort on a gurgle of laughter. "Just the thing to make a man really furious — and if you ask me, he wouldn't have thrown her a lifebelt today if she'd been going down for the third time!"

"No, it was odd, wasn't it? People are talking about them, you know. I suppose there can't be any truth in it, Mavis?"

Mavis shrugged. "I wouldn't know. But I wouldn't be surprised if I'd hit the nail on the head, even though I was joking. It was her week-end off, and they left together on Friday night. Harris saw them. Very suspicious . . . talking away like old friends and then he tossed her his car keys, and she tripped to his car with a sparkle in her eyes and her lips parted in anticipation. Nice goings-on for a surgeon and a Staff . . . I'd like to know what Matron would say if . . . "

"That will do, Nurse!" Honor had not known that her voice could drip with ice until this moment — but her cold fury came over with startling effect. Both girls leaped round guiltily, flushed and frightened and a little ashamed as they met that stern and uncompromising gaze. "If you were to concentrate on your work instead of maliciously speculating on the affairs of your seniors, your reports might be much better than they are at the moment. I have a very good mind to report you both to Sister — and I'm sure she would have as much contempt for your stupid, empty prattle as I have! Get on with your work — and don't let me catch you gossiping again!"

She turned on her heel and left them, the flush of anger in her cheeks, her eyes bright with the rushing tears of humilation that she had not dared to betray to her juniors. She had not overheard all their conversation but every word of those last remarks had reached her ears, chilling and horrifying her as she realised that herself and Calder Savage were under discussion.

She had not been severe enough — but she had dreaded an unconscious admission that she knew they were talking about her and Calder. It was easier and wiser to pretend complete ignorance of the matter under discussion and just upbraid them for gossiping on duty.

She knew that they were young and a little silly, first-year nurses doing their first turn of duty in Theatre, a little pleased and thrilled by the unusual atmosphere that existed between the staff. Neither did she forget that at their age she had not been averse to a little mischievous speculation about the imaginary affairs that went on between senior members of the staff.

But because it was her reputation that was being bandied about by a pair of silly girls, she was justifiably angry — and contemptuous of her own failure to deal competently with the matter. She knew very well that had they been discussing anyone but herself and Calder Savage, she would have censured them but passed over the matter within a few moments, making allowance for the love of idle gossip that existed to some extent in every human breast.

It scarcely seemed possible that anyone could misconstrue that incident on Friday night. But if those two juniors had made so much out of it, it was not unlikely that other tongues were busy. Honor shrank from the thought of facing curious eyes and fending off eager questions and knowing that people were talking about her when she was out of earshot.

She should never have allowed Calder to drive her home that evening. It was inevitable that someone should have seen them together — and her cheeks burned anew as the remembered her own faint surprise at the familiar way in which he had tossed over the car keys and the easy expectation of her acceptance of such familiarity.

Surely no one could really believe for a moment that she would be fool enough to involve herself with a senior surgeon in the way that those girls had implied! Surely no one could think for a moment that she would spend a week-end with the SSO! Surely no one could link the innocent coincidence that had provided them both with a free week-end at that particular time — and surely their reputations were not to be smeared because she had accepted his offer of a lift in his car!

She wondered if she was making too much of the mischievous chatter . . . but she had always guarded her reputation very jealously and she had learned in the early days of her training that reputations were easily lost in her profession simply because hospital life inevitably threw the sexes together in an atmosphere which insisted on scrupulous morality while providing innumerable opportunities for light flirtation and more dangerous affairs, and because gossip was the breath of life within the sterile, cold and unemotional walls of a hospital.

She could not afford to have her name linked with any member of the male staff let alone a senior surgeon, she thought in sudden panic. Matron was a strict and somewhat harsh disciplinarian of the old school and however excellent the record of any nurse on her staff she was swift to dismiss her if she suspected any relaxation of the moral code she maintained — and rightly so — to be the vital necessity in a nursing career. The SSO could not afford to have his name linked with a nurse, either . . . unless it was an open, straightforward affair with marriage as its aim and even that was frowned on despite the allowances that had to be made for a natural tendency for men and women to fall in love. The Hospital Committee who had appointed Calder Savage to their staff did not fail to share Matron's views in the matter of moral behaviour within or without the hospital precincts. A doctor or a surgeon had to be the most cautious and discreet of men, not only in his dealings with the patients but also in his contacts with the nursing staff. There were flirtations and affairs, of course — but the swiftest route to dismissal was by making such interest in the opposite sex the subject of common gossip.

Honor was thankful that the day was almost over and she could make her escape. She knew that if there was any gossip going the rounds of the hospital, Joy would have heard it and should waste no time in recounting it to her — not without a little malice — for while she constantly played with fire and had been singularly fortunate or sufficiently discreet to avoid Matron's censure so far, she had often teased

Honor about her 'unnatural attitude to the charms of all those lovely men'. Joy would not believe that there was any foundation for the gossip and it would amuse her that Honor's name should be bandied about so freely in such obvious error.

Abruptly, she realised that Calder might also be aware of the gossip — if any existed outside the heads of those silly juniors. Certainly it would explain his strange hostility of the day, and her own fury had every sympathy with his annoyance and distaste. It was impossible to tackle him on the matter, both pride and perception would stand in the way. After all, there might be no real gossip: he might not nave heard if their names were being linked so unpleasantly; he might have an entirely different reason for snubbing her as he had done — and he would not welcome a request for an explanation. Their friendship had been too short-lived to put them on such intimate terms that she could reproach him, admit that he had hurt her and ask him for his reasons.

Briefly she wandered if it was a deliberate policy to allay the gossip, carried just that little too far. But if that were the case, he would surely waste no time in conveying somehow an explanation and a plea for her understanding. In her heart, she knew that he would not seek her out, would not even write a letter to explain the matter. For some inexplicable reason, he had decided that friendship between them was out of the question. All the more strange a decision because they had parted so amicably the previous evening. She might never know why he had so abruptly ceased to feel any interest in her. She could only assume that he did know of the rumours that linked them, disliked and resented the talk and felt it wiser to end their friendship before it went any further. It had probably been too young, too light for him to feel any regret — she had merely been at hand when he needed someone to listen to his problems, someone to ease the feeling of depression and loneliness; and Honor told herself firmly that he would not have given her a second glance or a second thought if the circumstances had been different.

It was the only explanation. Search her memory and her conscience as she might, she could discover nothing that might have given him a personal dislike of her. She knew she had not driven him away, as another girl might have done, by an obvious attraction to him, by an overdone eagerness for his company or a smugly confident assumption that, given time, she would take Heather's place in his life. It was true that the liking she had for him was almost affection. It was also true that the faint hope of winning his love had stirred, for Honor knew that of all men in the world she could love Calder Savage with ease and delight. Fortunately, her heart was still her own. Perhaps it was as well that she would not be seeing him again outside Theatre, for certainly a few more weeks of knowing him and of being with him would have taken her over the verge of love, and then her hurt and dismay if he had ceased to seek her company would have been almost too great to bear.

It was better this way, disappointed though she was. And she would follow his lead. Not for Honor Portland the folly of running after a man who so obviously wanted no more of a circumstantial and admittedly unusual friendship. He would discover that while she was always courteous and pleasant when circumstances demanded that they meet and speak, she could be as cool and aloof as he wished.

Momentarily, she toyed with the idea of requesting a transfer from Theatre. But the idea was summarily dismissed. That would only be an admission that she was embarrassed and offended by his attitude, an admission that she no longer wanted to work with him and possibly an admission in the eyes of her colleagues that the rumours were based on fact. She enjoyed working in Theatre — she would not allow any man or any circumstances to deprive her of it while she felt she was giving her best to the arduous but enthralling demands of the work.

As a well trained and efficient nurse, she had learned to conceal her personal feelings on duty, learned to dismiss them while the care of a patient or the daily routine demanded complete concentration and attention to detail.

Off duty, she might allow herself to think of Calder, to recall the brief hours she had spent with him, to regret that she had come too late in his life and that when they had met his heart was fully preoccupied with another woman. But on duty he would merely be the SSO who commanded her respect and obedience and attention, without any personal involvement of thought or feeling . . .

★ ★ ★

Joy leaned forward to study the thick coating of mascara on her long lashes. "Well, I'm glad you decided to go, after all," she said absently.

Honor stepped into her dress and eased it over her hips. She slipped her arms through the thin straps and struggled to fasten the long zip at the back. "There isn't any point in wasting a perfectly good ticket," she returned carelessly.

"Here, let me do that!" Joy turned and grinned at her friend. "You'll do yourself an injury." Honor obediently moved towards her and turned her back so that Joy could pull up the zip. "I don't suppose he'll be there — and even if he is, what does it matter?" Joy went on with a faintly stern note in her voice. "Ignore him like a sensible girl!"

"He is going to the Ball, I heard him telling Duncan Grey. He's taking Sister Rawley."

"Good luck to him! I hope he may have a thoroughly miserable evening, and he will with that wet blanket!"

Honor shrugged. "I hope they'll both have a marvellous evening, then perhaps people will have something else to talk about next week," she said with more than a little bitterness.

"Never mind, ducky," Joy said soothingly. "It will blow over soon, anyway. It's a pity that wretched man ever came to Camhurst!"

Honor smiled reluctantly. "You thought he was the cat's whiskers until recently," she reminded her indignant friend.

"That was before he treated you so abominably! What on earth is wrong with the man? Why is he being so unpleasant to you, anyway?" There was a very natural curiosity behind the seemingly casual questions for Honor had not talked about those two meetings with Calder Savage. "If he's just angry at the gossip, he wants to remember that he was the one to instigate it. No one forced him to bring you home that night and he didn't have to take you out on the Sunday. Did he make a pass at you, Honor?"

"Of course not!" Honor rejected the suggestion so coldly that Joy obviously thought it wise to drop the subject.

"Oh, well, don't let him spoil your evening. There'll be plenty of men to occupy your thoughts tonight if you'll give them half a chance. It should be fun. We don't get many opportunities to let our hair down and even Matron will turn a blind eye tonight."

"Maybe, but she won't forget it if you behave too outrageously, Joy. Do be careful, won't you?"

Joy laughed. "Good heavens, child — one can't get into much mischief in the full view of at least a thousand eyes — and Brian is scarcely the type to sweep me off my feet, you know."

"He's calling for us in ten minutes — so move away from that mirror and let me do my face"

Joy sprayed her hair lavishly with lacquer and then reluctantly rose from the dressing-table. Honor slipped on to the vacated stool and rapidly made up her face while Joy vacillated between bedroom and sitting-room window in the hope that her escort and current boy friend would arrive on time for once.

St. Antony's Commemoration Ball was a gala occasion — the one night in the year when the hospital carried on with a skeleton staff and the others threw themselves wholeheartedly into an evening's revelry. The local ballroom was hired for the occasion, which was discussed for weeks beforehand and recalled nostalgically for weeks afterwards. Many a satisfactory romance had begun at the Commemoration Ball . . . and many a youthful nurse prepared for the evening with hopeful expectation bringing a flush to her cheeks and a sparkle to her eyes.

Brian and the friend he had provided

to act as escort for Honor were only a few minutes late and they arrived at the ballroom to be met by a confusion of vivid colours, of dark suits and white shirt-fronts, of swirling gowns and animated smiling faces, of lively intercourse between the dancers and those who watched them from the surrounding tables.

A long table was reserved for Matron, Assistant Matron, Home Sister and the Sister Tutors, members of the Hospital Committee, the consultants and senior staff — and it was noticeable that those who were within sight and hearing of these notables were more decorous than their more fortunate fellows. Fortunately for the general success of the evening, Matron and some of the others did not stay very long and things became livelier and more unconventional later in the evening.

Spirits were high for it was a night of gaiety and merriment. Honor and Joy were greeted rapturously by friends as they waited for their escorts and within a very few minutes they were installed at a table conveniently distant from the top table, reasonably near to the bar and not so close to the orchestra dais that conversation was stifled. They were a merry party and Joy was obviously delighting in the attentions and admiration of the men she had so skilfully drawn to her side. The orchestra was excellent, the dance floor was just right, the bar was carrying on a splendid trade and the youth and enthusiasm of the crowd ensured a noisy, lively evening.

Honor was given little opportunity to think about Calder Savage or even to look for him among the mass of dancers. She was a very good dancer and she did not lack for partners during the first part of the evening. Her spirits soared as she enjoyed a greater popularity than she had known during the last ten days. For she had been conscious of a certain coolness in the manner of her colleagues at St.

Antony's and she had been working under a strain. It was pleasant to relax, to enjoy herself, to forget the hospital, her work, Calder Savage and the gossip for a few brief hours.

It chanced that she was sitting out the last dance before the interval with a young man she did not know very well, a friend of Brian's who had joined their table at the beginning of the evening. He was pleasant enough but rather shy and he could not dance. They sat in silence for the most part, Honor absently twirling an empty glass between her fingers as she watched the moving mass of dancers Her feet itched to the lively rhythm of the quickstep but she was not loath to sit down for a few minutes.

Her companion was obviously ill at ease and after a few moments he rose to his feet. "Er . . . do you mind if I talk to a chap I know? I've been trying to contact him all day," he said awkwardly.

Honor shook her head, smiling, and

watched him make his way to the bar with obvious relief in the set of his shoulders. She wondered that he should be a friend of Brian, that happy-go-lucky extrovert — and then she reminded herself that it took all types to make a world. He would probably have been much happier spending the evening with his books and had only given in to the persuasions of his friends to buy a ticket for the Ball.

Joy swept past in Brian's arms, smiling and waving. Several glances turned towards Honor as she sat alone at the table and, suddenly feeling conspicuous, she picked up her evening bag and left her seat to go to the powder room. By the time she had powdered her nose and tidied up her hair, Joy and the others would be back.

As she entered the powder room, she was conscious of a sudden silence as she was recognised. Colour stole into her cheeks but she pretended to notice nothing, greeted the girls that she knew and crossed to a vacant mirror. The hubbub began again but it seemed to Honor that everyone was trying to avoid a previous topic of conversation. Telling herself that she was being ultra-sensitive, she busied herself with her lipstick.

One girl studied her with a faintly malicious smile. "It looks as though you've lost your boy friend, Portland — I've just seen him with Sister Rawley, dancing so close I couldn't have slipped a hairpin between them."

The colour deepened in Honor's face but she made no reply, snapping her compact closed with fingers that shook a little.

"Which boy friend is that, Janet?" another girl asked with a grin. "Oh, Portland doesn't have so many that she can afford to lose one," the tormentor retorted unkindly. "Particularly such an illustrious one as the SSO — it doesn't look as though you'll be offered any more week-ends with our handsome charmer. By the look of things, I'd say he's lining up Sister Rawley right now . . . "

"Oh, shut up, Janet," someone said rather curtly. "There's no need to be so beastly."

"Portland doesn't mind, do you?" Janet demanded. "After all, she wouldn't touch the SSO with a barge-pole these days." She chuckled. "He never gets close enough!"

Honor held on to her temper. It would be disastrously easy to flare up, to turn on her tormentor — but it would only instigate more gossip and certainly would not help matters. It was much better to ignore the spiteful jibes . . . Janet Finlay was noted for her malicious tongue and jealous nature and she had disliked Honor since their early training days.

Janet shrugged her shoulders as Honor continued to apply lipstick without giving any sign that she had heard the remarks. She turned away, disappointed. "Oh, come on!" she said impatiently to her friends. "I don't want to spend the entire evening in here, certainly not in present company, anyway!"

She marched from the powder room with her friends in her wake. The young nurse at the next mirror glanced sympathetically at Honor. "She's a nasty gossip," she said warmly. "There wouldn't have been so much talk if she hadn't spread it all over the hospital — and it was that friend of hers, Sheena Harris, who saw you with the SSO in the first place and couldn't wait to broadcast it.

Honor forced herself to smile. "They have to talk about someone . . . at least they're leaving someone else alone if they talk about me," she said with studied indifference.

"They've been giving you a rough time, haven't they?"

"Not particularly. I don't see very much of Janet Finlay or her cronies — that's one advantage of working in Theatre."

"Did you go out with the SSO?" the

nurse asked hesitantly. "I don't mean to pry into your affairs — but I'm not the only one who didn't believe a word of the gossip."

"We were seen leaving the hospital together — that seems to be enough for most people," Honor retorted bitterly. "That doesn't prove a thing!"

"If you must know, I went out with him once — that's all. He took me into the country and we had lunch at a pub — I was home by six o'clock. I suppose that's ample evidence for people like Janet Finlay that we were having an affair — but it was never anything of the kind!"

"Well, I think that is your business even if you were having an affair with the SSO or anyone else — and it's a pity that Finlay and a few others I could mention haven't anything better to do than slander a perfectly respectable nurse!" She was silent for a few moments, regarding Honor's reflection in the mirror. Then she rushed on: "I suppose you know that he isn't getting married, after all — and that people are saying it's all your fault?"

Honor paused in the act of dosing her bag and her fingers tightened over the thin velvet material. "My fault!" she echoed.

"Well, the rumour is that his fiancée got to know about the gossip and believed it enough to break their engagement. Anyway, it's all off — that I do know."

Honor's teeth clenched on her underlip. Now she understood why so many of her colleagues had cold-shouldered her during the last few days. Calder Savage had gained a swift popularity with the nursing staff and every woman loves a wedding. If they believed that she was indirectly to blame for his broken engagement — and it was typical, she thought with grim irony, that the man was never blamed even though he might have been disloyal to his fiancee, which was not the case where Calder was concerned as far as she knew — certainly she had not aided and abetted him to be false to the woman he loved! But if they believed that she was to blame then her fellow nurses would be angry and disgusted and inclined to shun her company and their attitude would be justified if it was true. But it was not true — and it was too bad that a perfectly innocent friendship, particularly one so short-lived, should have such unpleasant repercussions.

Her sympathiser looked at that set face and stony eyes and decided she had said not only enough but possibly too much. "Well, I must be getting back to my escort or he'll think I've run out on him," she said hastily.

Honor nodded absently and scarcely saw the girl go. She was alone at last and she stared at her reflection, noticing the angry spots of colour in her cheeks, the suspicious wetness of her eyes — furious with herself for caring so much and determined not to give away to the threatening tears. She would not allow a handful of spiteful girls to ruin an evening that had been enjoyable until she decided to visit the powder room. She would not allow all those curious and hostile eyes to see that she cared for their opinion of her. And she would die rather than allow Calder Savage to know that he was the cause of the greatest heartache and humilation she had ever known.

She bent her head, gripping her bag so tightly that her knuckles were white with the strain. It would not matter so much if he had not stormed the citadel of her heart so unexpectedly . . . she could shrug off the unpleasantness in the confidence that it would soon be forgotten — if only she hadn't fallen in love with a man who had developed a sudden indifference to her. For she did love him. She had not dared to admit it to herself until now, but she loved him and her hurt was all the greater because she had given her heart without invitation or encouragement. It was the greatest folly that anyone could commit — to fall in love so abruptly and without good reason when every instinct insisted the futility and stupidity of loving a man who would never, never think of her in that light.

She had never loved anyone before. Why had Fate decreed that she should love Calder? Why had life been so unkind as to bring him in her path when there could never be any fulfilment or response for that love? Why did it have to be Calder Savage — a man who was not only deeply in love with a woman who no longer wanted him but also a man who had proved that his promise of friendship was not to be trusted, that his nature was vacillatory and unpredictable, that he was prone to regretted impulses and guilty of kindling an emotion he had no intention of encouraging?

He was not entirely to blame. He could not know that she would fall headlong in love with him on the strength of a few brief hours in his company. She had invited his friendship and his confidences, perhaps she had unconsciously betrayed an emotion he did not welcome on that fateful Sunday and that was the reason for his sudden change of manner; his obvious avoidance of her company and conversation, the deliberate and seemingly unkind coldness of his attitude was in such marked contrast to his former friendliness and warmth and sympathy.

Honor stifled a sob. All the tears in the world would not retrieve her heart or ease the hurt and humiliation. She could only call pride to the rescue and avoid any chance betrayal of her feelings to anyone, and she could even he thankful that Calder had ended their association for he must never know that she loved him, never suspect that he had come to mean so much to her in so short a time.

Joy came into the room like a whirlwind. "There you are! I couldn't think what had happened to you . . . " She broke off, startled and dismayed by the naked pain in her friend's eyes. "Are you all right, ducky?" she asked gently, slipping an arm about Honor's waist.

Honor nodded. It was an effort to smile, to speak naturally, to shrug off the vast desolation that seemed to occupy her whole being. "Except for a shiny nose," she said brightly.

Joy cast a critical eye over her face. "Looks all right to me," she said suspiciously.

"It is now!" Honor retorted with forced gaiety. "But I could almost see my face in it!"

Joy frowned. "Are you sure there's nothing wrong? I saw that wretch had deserted you. Did you hate sitting on your own?"

"Of course not, and there's nothing wrong, believe me. I'm having a marvellous evening and I shall be sorry when it comes to an end."

Joy hugged her. "Good girl! You're the life and soul of the party. There were groans all round when we thought you'd decided to go home. I don't know why I didn't think of the powder

166

room sooner. Come on, ducky, there's a drink waiting for you and the dancing will start again in a few minutes."

They left the powder room together but in the crush of people in the narrow lane between the tables, they were soon separated. Honor was in front and she glanced back to look for Joy, missed her in the crowd and turned to make her way to their table, leaving her to follow.

Her heart leaped into her throat as she came face to face with Calder Savage. It was impossible to ignore him, for a sudden surge of humanity almost thrust her into his arms. He steadied her with a hand at her elbow and smiled briefly as she murmured her thanks. She wondered that she could find her voice at all but it came out with only the faintest of tremors that he could not have noticed in the hubbub.

"Enjoying yourself?" he asked politely, gazing at some distant spot above her head. "Very much," she said with lively emphasis. "I adore dancing."

"You're young," he said, deliberately patronising. "When you get to my age you'll see very little point in romping about a dance-floor to music — but I like to see young people having a good time." With a courteous nod and a smile that failed to touch his dark eyes, he passed on, leaving her to teeter momentarily between love and hate.

Joy caught up with her and grabbed her arm "What did he say?" she demanded eagerly, consumed with curiosity.

"Nothing more than he could avoid," Honor retorted curtly.

"Beast!" Joy turned to glare indignantly at the retreating back of the offender.

As the girls got back to their table, the MC announced a Paul Jones. In the general scramble that followed, Honor found herself dancing with Brian. The dance soon came to an end, and to her dismay, Honor found she was facing Duncan Grey. The young anaesthetist had obviously had a little too much to drink, and as his hand dropped on her shoulder to claim the next dance, he lurched and laughed loudly.

Her grey eyes widened anxiously, then to her relief, she saw Calder Savage making his way towards them. "Mind if I cut in," he said pleasantly. He detached Duncan firmly. "Go and douse your head, you idiot!" he said quietly and then moved away with Honor in his arms to the slow, dreamy rhythm of the waltz.

She would not have danced with him if she could have avoided notice by walking away as he rescued her from Duncan Grey. But now she delighted in the embrace of his arm, the clasp of his hand, the nearness of him, and she gave herself up to the pleasure of the dance and temporarily dismissed all other considerations from her mind.

"Thank you . . . " she said, a little shyly.

"My pleasure," he returned lightly. "You dance very well."

"It isn't difficult with a good partner,"

she told him, somewhat stiffly, embarrassed by the unexpected compliment. "I didn't expect you to join in a Paul Jones," she added, a little pointedly, remembering his scathing remarks of earlier in the evening. "I thought you considered yourself too old for dancing."

He smiled faintly. "Ah, yes — but Mr. Grey reminded me that I'm not yet in my dotage." He added, surprisingly: "Perhaps I hoped for the chance to dance with you, Honor."

She stiffened in his arms. "Perhaps you haven't noticed that my table isn't so very far from yours," she retorted. "You didn't have to wait for a Paul Jones!"

"I didn't like to intrude, and I never did care for queuing."

"You wouldn't be dancing with me now if Mr. Grey hadn't made himself so conspicuous," she told him bluntly.

"I'd forgotten how perceptive you are," he said, glancing down at her with a smile in his eyes.

She would not respond to the warmth of that smile. She looked back at him coldly. "You've chosen to forget a great many things," she said stonily.

"Is that an accusation?" He continued to smile but his eyes had hardened.

"Merely a reminder."

"You're referring to my indifference recently, of course. You brought it on yourself, you silly girl," he said impatiently.

"Don't be so darned patronising!" she flared and wrenched herself free from his arms just as the music ended. She would have stalked away from him but he caught her wrist. "Do you mind?" she asked pointedly, glaring at his detaining hand.

"Certainly. There's enough talk without creating a scene on the dance-floor," he said sternly.

"I'm trying to avoid comment. The Paul Jones is beginning again, Mr. Savage."

"I've had enough. Let me get you a drink." And he urged her gently off the floor, his easy smile lulling any suspicions that might have stirred among the spectators.

As soon as they were absorbed by the throng, she pulled her wrist away and turned on him angrily. "I don't want a drink, thank you. In fact, I don't want to be seen in your company. It's caused quite enough gossip already, in my opinion."

"Nonsense! This is an occasion, etiquette is relaxed tonight and there isn't any reason why we shouldn't enjoy a friendly drink together." He added quietly: "I want to talk to you."

Their eyes met for a long moment. Then she shrugged. "Oh, very well," she agreed reluctantly.

She stood watching the dancers while he procured the drinks, wondering at the sudden change. Half an hour before, he had been as remote and cold as any stranger; she appreciated that he had rescued her from Duncan Grey merely to save her from embarrassment and that he would have done the same for

172

any girl in the ballroom. It would be balm for her aching heart if she could believe that a few turns about the floor with her in his arms had caused him to regret their estrangement, but she would not fool herself that she meant anything to him. He was merely being politely pleasant, and perhaps he had mellowed in the atmosphere of the evening. She could not imagine why he should wish to talk to her when he had made it obvious of late that he would prefer to have nothing to do with her.

Why had he told her that she was to blame for the talk that their brief friendship had aroused? Why had he called her a silly girl? Why, oh why, had he been so unfriendly, so distant, so chilling entirely without cause — she could not think of anything she might have said or done to offend or anger him!

He joined her and offered her the glass of lager. "Something cool and long, I thought; dancing can be thirsty work," he said lightly.

"Thank you." She sipped the ice-cold lager. "Sister Rawley won't like being deserted, you know," she told him with faint malice.

"I doubt if I'll be missed for a few minutes," he returned carelessly. He looked down at her steadily. "I did hope to escort you tonight, you know."

"That must have been one of those things you preferred to forget," she said bitingly.

"Not exactly. Look, don't bite my head off, Honor. I didn't let my tongue run away with me!"

She stared at him. "I don't know what you mean."

"Then think about it!"

"Are you accusing me of something?" she asked slowly.

"Of talking too much!"

"About us, do you mean?" She was staggered.

He gestured impatiently. "So I spent an evening with you, and drove down the High Street that Sunday in the hope of seeing you. That doesn't put us on a level of intimacy. It didn't mean anything, you know. I'm sorry if you thought otherwise, but I thought of you as a friend and nothing more. It isn't my fault if you chose to imagine that you were going to catch me on the rebound."

Colour swept into her face and then receded abruptly, leaving her pale and shocked. "You're either unbalanced or disgustingly conceited, Mr. Savage," she flared. "I imagined nothing of the kind. I wouldn't want you on the rebound or any other way, believe me! No wonder you've avoided me like the plague! Don't worry — you've nothing to fear from me. I haven't the slightest interest in you — and I'll thank you to kill the rumour that I'm to blame for your broken engagement. It was nothing to do with me — and I'm not going to be held responsible. The next time you want someone to hold your hand while you pour out your troubles you'd better find someone who isn't fool enough to think you need a friend! Because that's the only thought that crossed my mind — and I very much regret that I've got such a soft spot for lame dogs! Good night, Mr. Savage!"

Honor placed her almost untouched drink on a near-by table and walked away from him before he could frame any reply. She heard him call her name but she ignored it and pushed her way through the crowd with seething impatience. She had never been so angry, so humiliated, so shocked in all her life. How could she have been such a fool as to think herself in love with him? She hated and despised him . . . the conceited, self-satisfied brute! To think that any intelligent man could leap to such ridiculous conclusions! Honor could scarcely believe that he had said such things. How dared he accuse her of discussing him with her friends — for that was what his suspicions amounted to! How dared he assume that her interest in him went beyond friendship and liking! How amazing that he should panic and decide to give her no further cause to believe that his interest held any personal emotion, not that she had believed it for a moment but it was obvious that he had thought so. She must have unconsciously betrayed the depth of her liking for him on that Sunday! She had been too much at ease with him, too swift to further the sense of intimacy he had evoked, too easy and undemanding a companion, and he must have construed her warm friendliness and sympathy and understanding as evidence that she was strongly attracted to him. Well, that was no crime, but it was humiliating to discover that she had frightened him off quite unconsciously merely because she was sorry for him, because she liked him, because she welcomed his friendship!

At least she knew now why he had changed so abruptly. She would no longer need to puzzle over it. But she would have given anything to be able to turn back the clock, knowing what she knew now. She would not be such a fool again. She would snub that kindly offer of a lift and maintain a strictly impersonal relationship with a senior surgeon.

Her cheeks were still flaming when she rejoined her party. Joy looked at her curiously. "What happened to you? I thought you were joining in the Paul Jones."

"I changed my mind," she said briefly. "Look, Joy — I think I'll go home. I've a beastly headache and it's so noisy here."

Joy narrowed her eyes. "That wretched man has upset you! I'd like to give him a piece of my mind! I don't know why you care so much, ducky — he isn't worth it, you know!"

Honor forced herself to laugh. "Don't be silly! It has nothing to do with the SSO. It isn't his fault if I've developed a bad headache. I don't care a snap of my fingers for him, idiot. Goodness knows why you should think otherwise!"

"Hm! I have my reasons," Joy retorted cryptically. "Do you really want to go home? I'll come with you." And she picked up her bag and half-rose to her feet.

Honor pressed her back into her seat. "No need for you to sacrifice your evening. I'll be all right. Make my excuses to the others, will you?"

She hurried to get her coat from the cloakroom before Joy could protest any further. She was impatient to escape — and terrified of meeting Calder Savage again that night.

6

CALDER could not shake off the feeling that he had handled things badly. He realised that it had been a mistake to approach Honor in such a way, and he was puzzled by her reaction. It had contained no hint of guilt. His implications had shocked and angered her — and it had surprised him that she was capable of the tirade she had thrown at his head. He had smashed the quiet serenity and found a little virago. But he could scarcely blame her if he had misjudged her, and it seemed that he had.

Perhaps she had not talked too freely about their association. Perhaps the rumours had started simply because they had been seen together for a few brief moments, or because Honor's flat-mate had seen him leaving on that Friday evening and leaped to conclusions that she could not resist broadcasting. It did not take much for gossip to get out of hand.

Obviously he had blamed Honor quite unfairly, and she had every right to resent his accusations and his attitude of late. After all, she had offered him an unemotional friendliness, a sympathy and an understanding, a valuable perception and comfort, and he had been fool enough to distort her motives and lose a good friend in the process. They would never be friends now and it shook him a little to realise the depth of his disappointment and sense of loss.

He took himself severely to task, recalling the many times he had snubbed her and probably hurt her, the pointed coldness of his attitude, the unreasonable anger he had known when he believed that she was responsible for the gossip. Supposing she had been attracted to him, had hoped that their friendship might lead to a warmer emotion between them — there was nothing wrong in such attraction, such hopes. It was perfectly natural for a young woman to feel emotional interest in a man who had shown that he liked her company and appreciated her warm friendliness. She was scarcely to be blamed for liking him, and what kind of a fool was he to resent the liking of an attractive and pleasant girl?

Most men in his position, jilted by the woman he loved and hoped to marry, would have been only too grateful for the reassurance provided by the interest of another woman. It came as a slight shock to realise that he had scarcely given Heather a thought since that abortive trip to London. He had expected to feel regret and continued heartache. Instead, he had been so absorbed in his work, so much in demand socially and so incensed by the rumours that linked his name with Honor Portland, that the combination had successfully driven Heather from his mind — and his heart, too, he admitted quite frankly. No doubt he had loved her at the beginning of their long and frustrating affair. But he knew now that he had continued to love her from habit alone, and it had taken very little to open his eyes to the fact that he was not in love with Heather. Her decision to break with him had seemed a drastic and painful step at the time but he was able to admit now that Heather's wisdom and perception and integrity were greater than his own. Whether or not she loved him still, she had known that marriage between them was out of the question — and he could be grateful to her now for following her instincts.

He thought wryly that, unpleasant though the last ten days or so had been, they had wrought a cure. They had given him something else to think about and prevented him from brooding over the loss of Heather and deceiving himself that his life was empty without her. He had been cured of that fanciful emotion he had named love, and Honor had played her part in that cure.

The thought of Honor stirred his compassion and he determined to make his peace with her as soon as possible. It might well be that his actions had given her a dislike of him and that they would never get back to that easy, warm relationship which had sprung to life so abruptly and been killed with equal abruptness by his own hand. But he would only have himself to blame if that was the case.

He wanted Honor's friendship; more than that, he wanted her affection and loyalty. He had been exceptionally foolish and his stupidity might have cost him the one thing he wanted now that it was out of reach — her liking. She might even have come to love him in time, and as the fanciful thought struck into his mind, he realised that his entire attitude had sprung from disappointment and that he had unconsciously recognised in Honor Portland the embodiment of all he wanted in a woman. If the wish to keep her by his side, to depend on her strength and comfort, to cherish the almost incredible rapport that existed between them, was love, then he loved Honor in a way that he had never loved Heather. Love could leap to life so swiftly, so naturally — he did not doubt that for a moment but he had never believed that it could happen to him. Yet it seemed that it had happened and he faced the astonishing realisation that he loved and wanted Honor more than he had wanted anything in the whole of his life.

This was no sudden storm of emotion but a quiet confident acceptance of the rightness of his love. He realised that only Honor could have broken through the proud barrier he had erected about his vulnerable emotions. He believed implicitly that every day of his life had been spent on a path that had eventually and inevitably brought him to the point of meeting and loving the gentle, perceptive girl who had invaded his heart and his mind so delicately and yet so irrevocably.

Facing the truth with absolute honesty and courage, he admitted that his pride had denied him all the things that his heart might have sought. He had been consciously proud of himself and his own efforts, proud of his dedication to surgery and his determination to succeed to the point of obsession. He had been too proud to relinquish his freedom, even to Heather who had meant a great deal to him in the early days of their romance. He had been too proud to take a chance on marriage, fearful of failure, insisting that a settled income and a satisfactory position in his profession and the prestige that went with it would provide more certainty of success in marriage, blinding himself to the truth that if he loved enough he need not fear failure or disappointment or any problems that might arise.

Unconsciously, he had loved Honor from the first — and again pride was to blame for the loss of her friendship. He had resented being the subject of hospital gossip and feared that its implications might affect his career. His pride had insisted that he was not a man to be discussed by gossip-mongers or to lower his standards by associating with a mere Staff Nurse who could not be trusted to keep a still tongue in her head. His pride had urged him to snub her, to withdraw his warm friendliness, to punish her for embroiling him in a spate of spiteful comment. It had blinded him to her point of view, to justice and common sense.

Well, pride had had its day, and he was finished with it. For where love burned, pride could not survive. Love was the only cure for pride — and he loved Honor enough to humble himself to win her love. He would have no doubts about the future if he could persuade her to marry him. He would even welcome the demands and the required adjustments that his pride had never allowed him to accept in the past.

But his thoughts were leaping ahead too rapidly and he forced himself to apply the rein. Honor was angry and hostile. Why should she believe at the moment that they were destined to meet and love and share the future? She might never believe it. After all, he had done nothing to merit her love or even her liking — and he must face the unpalatable fact that he had come to terms with himself too late to know personal happiness in life. He had behaved abominably to Honor and it would be a just punishment if he failed to redeem himself in her eyes. But he intended to try, and pride would not get in the way. For Honor had become the lodestar of his life, of vital importance to his happiness, claiming priority even before his love for surgery — and he would do everything in his power to win back her friendship, her liking and her respect and hope with all his heart that in time he might win her love . . .

* * *

It was with this heartfelt determination that he set off for St. Antony's on the following morning. He had spent a virtually sleepless night for his head and his heart had been in turmoil, but there was an alertness and a confidence in his bearing as he mounted the steps of the hospital and an unusual friendly warmth in his greeting to the porter.

He had no operating list that day and there seemed little likelihood of seeing Honor. He told himself that it was just as well. Her anger would probably still be aflame and there was little he could say to her at this stage. He could not risk an apology being spurned by a justifiably indignant girl.

The day seemed to drag but he forced himself to concentrate on his work. It was such an effort that it was further proof that Honor was of more importance, and he could feel compassion for Heather who had hoped for so long that one day she might be of such primary importance to him. He understood at last the frustration and anxiety and bewilderment she must have known when he continued to give most of his emotions and energies to his career and failed to appreciate the value of the love she offered him. Heather had been very good to him and he was grateful, but he had found it impossible to love her as deeply and completely as marriage would demand for a man of his nature. Yet he had inexplicably given his heart to a girl he scarcely knew so entirely and so irrevocably that he had no thoughts for the future that did not include having Honor by his side.

He walked into Theatre the next day with a heart that hammered as though he were a schoolboy in the throes of calf love.

Duncan Grey greeted him with a grin. "Goodness, you were past the point of no return the other night, weren't you?"

Calder smiled faintly. "Was I? Sounds like the pot calling the kettle black!"

"Cutting me out and telling me to

take a damper! You must want to set the whole place talking about you and that nurse. Mind you, she's a pleasant little thing, although I've always found her rather uncompromising. No flirt, that one. I suppose that's why everyone went to town when she set her cap at you!"

"Did she set her cap at me?" he echoed dryly. "I think it might surprise you to hear that it was the other way about."

Grey whistled softly through his teeth. "So I've heard . . . and she gave you the brush-off."

Calder's eyes narrowed. "You've heard more than I have, apparently. It always amazes me that gossip-mongers are so adept at distorting the facts."

"Well, you should know the truth of the matter," Grey retorted unabashed.

"I do," he replied with some coolness and went on his way to the changing-room.

He made a point of entering the

Theatre where he was due to operate in the company of an assistant. He did not want his greeting for Honor to be too marked and it would be easier to smile absently, wish her good morning and then continue his conversation with Prentiss. He could have spared himself the carefully-planned caution for Honor was not in sight and did not enter the Theatre until some minutes later.

He was talking to Sister when she entered and a few moments later he turned to the table and the unconscious patient. It was a particularly difficult and skilful piece of operating and he forgot her in his complete absorption in the task.

The operation finally completed and the patient removed to the ward, Calder ripped off his mask and gloves and expelled tension with a sigh. It was invariably his custom to thank each member of the team for their combined assistance and efficiency and when he had done so, he moved towards the door. Passing Honor, he paused to speak to her.

"Thank you, Staff Nurse, everything was most satisfactory."

Her smile was cool and perfunctory. "No need to thank me for doing my job, sir."

"But you did it so efficiently and unobtrusively," he said appreciatively.

"Training counts, sir." She turned away from him and assiduously bent her mind to her task.

He could not mistake the rebuff and with a faint frown touching his eyes, he went to change. It was obvious that it would take time and patience to reestablish himself with Honor, and it was very probable that he would never do so. She might be transferred to another department at any time and then he would lose all opportunity of contact, for they were not likely to meet socially and he could scarcely force chance meetings upon her outside the hospital.

It was going to be very difficult,

and it did not come easily to him to stifle the pride which urged him to stop making a fool of himself, to face the fact that she was indifferent to him, to look about for someone else who might welcome his attentions and affections. But his love for Honor was very strong despite its precarious foundations — and he conquered the proud impulse and mentally retorted that he would be a greater fool to give up trying for the happiness that was so important to him.

As he let himself into the house on Oaklands Drive with the passing thought that he really would have to do something about decorating and furnishing the place, he stooped to collect the pile of letters that awaited him. He glanced idly through them as he made his way into the sitting-room to switch on the electric fire. His hand checked as he recognised a familiar handwriting, and he frowned as he ripped open the envelope, tossing the others on to a table. What the devil could Heather be writing to him about now?

She had covered a great many pages and it was obvious from the sprawling untidiness, so out of character, that she had written the words under some emotional stress.

It did not take him long to confirm the suspicion which had leaped to life at the endearment with which she began her letter. It was not like Heather to plead for anything, but this was a passionate and desperate appeal for a reconciliation. She insisted that she did love him, had always loved him and claimed that she must have been mad to think that she could live without him. She begged for his understanding and forgiveness and regretted the hurt she had inflicted on him. She asked him to make an arrangement for them to meet as soon as possible and hinted that they might be able to set a date for an early wedding.

Calder crumpled the letter, dismayed and confused. It was the last thing he had expected — and the last thing he wanted now. It was not going to be easy to compose a reply for she would inevitably be hurt — and enough of the old affection lingered for him to be reluctant to cause her distress.

It did not occur to him even momentarily that they could make a fresh start, that be might be wise to ignore his feeling for Honor and return to the woman he knew so 'well' the woman who knew and understood him as few people did. It was impossible for him to deny the way he felt about Honor — and it was unthinkable that he should marry anyone else. If he could not marry Honor then he would remain a bachelor for the rest of his life!

But he could not understand what had prompted Heather to write that letter. Was it possible that she had realised the futility and emptiness of pride? Was it true that she loved him and had never undergone the change of heart she had claimed such a short time before? Could she love him and say such things to him, stabbing at his heart and his pride and his self-respect? Had there been a motive behind her action or had she merely been going through a temporary lack of emotion?

His mouth twisted wryly as he recalled that Honor had prophesied this very thing. She had tried to comfort him with the assurance that Heather would probably regret the breaking of their engagement before very long, and she had been proved right. Would she be pleased if she knew or was there the faintest possible hope that she might know a pang of dread at the thought of his marriage to another woman now that she had known his friendship and his warmth, however fleeting?

He wished he knew the answer to that question. But he did know that he could not respond to Heather's appeal, could never agree to the hinted suggestion that they should be married after all. It would be kinder to make another trip to London to explain matters to Heather. But while he was reluctant to do that he was equally reluctant to bend his mind to the task of phrasing a letter to her.

Perhaps he would leave it for a few days. She would expect him to answer immediately, no doubt, but he needed time to marshal his thoughts. He also needed to talk to Honor, he thought grimly, and he would have to risk the possibility of betraying the emotions that were playing havoc with his heart and mind . . .

Later that evening, he dialled the telephone number of Honor's flat. He waited with some impatience and a thumping heart while the ringing tone echoed interminably in his ears. At last the familiar click of a lifted receiver replaced the irritating sound and a voice he did not recognise gave the number. Forcing himself to calmness, he asked for Miss Portland.

"I'm afraid she's out. Who's speaking?"

"You don't happen to know where she is, I suppose? It's rather important," he said and heard himself pleading for the information with some wry amusement.

"I'm sorry, I don't know. But if I can give her a message . . . ?"

"It doesn't matter. I'll ring again."

"I don't know what time she'll be in . . . wouldn't it be easier if you gave me your name and number? I could ask her to call you when she comes in." There was blatant curiosity behind her seemingly helpful words.

"Thank you, but . . . "

"That isn't Mr. Savage, by any chance?" The question seemed to be blurted impulsively.

Calder grimaced. "Why should it be?" he retorted rather impatiently, quite unconscious that he betrayed his identity by the very phrasing of his answer.

"Oh, just a thought. You'll ring again, then?"

"Yes, thank you." He replaced the receiver abruptly, scowling. He did not doubt that his interrogator had been

Honor's flat-mate. He did not think she was likely to have recognised his voice for he had never spoken to her, to his knowledge. But it was odd that she should have demanded if he were Calder Savage in just that tone of voice. He shrugged; it was immaterial if she did know that he was the caller so reluctant to give his name. If he had his way, it would not be very long before the whole of St. Antony's was aware of his strictly honourable intentions towards a Theatre nurse. That would give the gossips something to occupy their tongues!

★ ★ ★

Calder was sitting over coffee and wondering how soon he should telephone Honor when the doorbell shrilled. He went swiftly to answer it on a sudden leap of hope, and he stared in complete amazement at the immaculate and supremely beautiful Heather. His amazement was so obvious that she coloured slightly as she smiled up at him.

"Surprised?" she asked unnecessarily.

"Flabbergasted," he replied honestly. "What are you doing in Camhurst?"

"I'm calling on you, obviously," she returned flippantly.

"Come in," he said belatedly, stepping back.

"So this is the house," Heather said, looking about her with interest. "Very nice, but you always did have excellent taste, darling."

"It wasn't a question of taste, it was virtually the only suitable house on the market at a price I wanted to pay," he disclaimed. He led the way into the sitting-room. He did not doubt why she had come on impulse to see him, but he found it hard to hide his dismay and he dreaded the conversation that must ensue. "Sorry it's so untidy — but I'm pigging it at the moment," he said as lightly as he could.

Heather raised an eyebrow in

amusement. "Pigging it! My dear Calder!"

"Sorry, that comes of mixing too much with a certain Duncan Grey, anaesthetist. He's a decent chap but much addicted to slang and almost too juvenile for his age to be normal. A retarded adolescent, in fact — as I'm always telling him."

"St. Antony's seems to be very different from our experience of hospitals," she said sweetly but there was a faint edge to her voice.

"Let me pour you some coffee and then you can tell me how you came to be in Camhurst. I could scarcely believe my eyes, you know."

Heather pushed a stack of medical journals from a chair and sat down, watching him pour the coffee.

She took the cup from him and smiled her thanks. "I had some days due to me so I asked for leave and came to see you on the spur of the moment. You don't mind, I hope?"

"My dear, I'm delighted to see you,"

he said, trying to inject warm sincerity into the words.

She studied the coffee thoughtfully. "Then you've read my letter?"

His smile faded abruptly. His eyes were troubled as they met her gaze. "Yes, I've read it, and it was a great surprise."

"But not an unpleasant one, surely? I've been all kinds of a fool, I know — but I do love you and I take back all I said about not wanting to marry you." There was deliberate confidence in the tilt of her chin, in the warmth of her eyes and the faint smile that curved her lips, an expectancy that he found difficult to thwart.

He moved restlessly, placing an ashtray closer to her hand and bringing out his cigarette ease. "I'm sorry, darling," he said as gently as possible, looking down at her with compassion in his eyes.

She stiffened. "What do you mean?" Her voice was harsh, almost accusing.

"I mean that it's too late," he said quietly.

She placed her coffee cup on the table with careless disregard for its fragility. "So there is some truth in all the talk about you and a Staff Nurse!" she exclaimed angrily.

His eyes narrowed. "What do you know about that, Heather? I can't believe that a trivial snippet of local gossip could reach all the way to London!"

Her shoulders lifted in a shrug that implied contempt. She was furious and did not care that he knew it. "A friend of mine has a cousin at St Antony's."

"So you heard that I was supposedly involved with a Theatre Nurse, and that brought about a sudden change in your feelings?" There was a faintly cynical lift to his eyebrow.

"What on earth did you think you were doing?" she demanded. "You, a surgeon with your qualifications and position and a reputation to consider — to fool about with a silly chit

204

of a junior! What happened to that ridiculous pride of yours, Calder? Don't tell me a pretty face can make you forget your position at this stage in your career!"

The unmistakable sneer brought his own anger to boiling point but he kept a firm rein on his temper. Nothing could be gained by quarrelling with Heather. "I fail to see that it matters to you what I do, my dear," he said quietly. "We were finished before I even spoke to Honor Portland."

"Don't be a fool! Surely you didn't really believe that I wasn't going to marry you, I've waited eight years to be your wife, Calder — and no stupid little Staff Nurse is going to disappoint me now!"

He stared. "But your letter, the things you said when I came to London . . . "

"I thought your emotions needed a bit of a shake-up," she told him tartly. "I was fed up with being a habit, and I wasn't going to marry a man who only thought about me when he wasn't pre-occupied with his work. I decided that I'd make you think about me, make you realise that I meant more than your work to you, make you aware of what you'd be losing if I didn't marry you."

"I see," he said quietly. "You wanted to humble me. Perhaps if I'd loved you your plan would have worked. I find it difficult to believe that you could be so cold-blooded about our engagement, but I can't blame you for trying to find out how much I loved you — or if I loved you at all. As it happened, you clarified things for me, too."

Dismay and incredulity were replacing her anger now. "You can't mean that you don't want to marry me, Calder?" she asked blankly. Suddenly she caught at his hand. "You must marry me — I love you! I'm not too proud to plead for my happiness — and I can't lose you now. You mean too much to me . . . . "

He was embarrassed despite his

compassion. "It's impossible," he said gently. "I'm hoping to marry someone else."

She looked up at him bleakly. "That nurse?"

He nodded, a little reluctantly. She closed her eyes as if against a shaft of pain "But I don't suppose you've known her more than a few weeks!" she protested.

"Less than that," he admitted.

She was silent for a moment. Then she said hopelessly: "I think that hurts most of all, Calder, that you want to marry a girl you scarcely know — and yet I gave you eight years of my life and you never really wanted to marry me." She released his hand and rose to her feet. "I can't argue against that, I can't fight that sort of competition, Calder. I always knew you didn't really love me. I don't know why it should be a shock to hear you admit it."

"I haven't played fair with you . . . " he began regretfully.

She interrupted him. "What does

that matter now? I loved you and I was content with things as they were. You'd have married me years ago if I'd forced your hand but I didn't want you on those terms. I didn't have to go on loving and hoping. I could have broken with you when I first realised that you'd never want to marry me."

"But I would have married you!"

"And it would have been a mistake," she told him bluntly. "You would probably have fallen just as hard for someone eventually as you have for this girl you want to marry. It's the way it was meant to be, I suppose — and I'd rather have it like this than have known the happiness of being your wife only to lose you to someone else eventually." She added with some malice: "And think what a divorce would have done for your career, Calder, although I suppose you're enough in love now not to care if your work suffers because of a girl you scarcely know."

"Yes, I think I am," he said quietly.

"Only think, Calder?" she mocked

him gently. "You should be sure."

"I am sure," he said firmly. "Honor means more than my career or my reputation."

She nodded. "I thought she might," she said flatly and held out her hand. "Good-bye, Calder, be happy."

"I'll keep in touch," he said quickly, pressing her slender fingers with affectionate warmth.

She smiled a little wryly. "That would be a little too unconventional, even for the new Calder Savage," she told him.

Calder insisted on driving her to the hotel where she had booked a room and then, finding himself within a few minutes of Honor's address, made for the nearest telephone.

Again Joy answered the strident summons. "Honor? I'm afraid she's out. Oh, is that Mr. Savage again?"

He no longer cared that she knew his identity. "Yes, and it really is urgent. Are you sure you haven't any idea where . . ."

"But isn't she with you?" Joy asked in surprise.

"With me? No."

"Well, she went tearing out of here over an hour ago — on her way to see you," Joy told him. "Have you been at home all evening?"

"I'm in the High Street at the moment, but I was at the house until half an hour ago."

"Looks like you've missed each other. She might have had a long wait for a bus, you know — and arrived just after you left."

He cursed beneath his breath. "Now what?" He spoke to himself in helpless dismay.

"Well, she'll come back here if she doesn't find you in. Why not ring her again later?" Joy suggested.

But Calder scarcely heard her. He had recognised the slim, slow-walking figure in the distance and with an abrupt thanks, he slammed down the receiver and left the call-box. He strode along the pavement towards Honor who had her hands thrust in the pockets of her dark raincoat and her chin slumped on her chest as she stared at the wet pavement and ignored the slight drizzle of rain that was touching her hair with sparkling lights in the street lighting.

Calder reached her and halted a few feet away. She looked up, startled, as he blocked her way.

For a moment or two, nothing existed in the world but their two selves as they looked into each other's eyes, searching, hoping, longing. Calder knew a surge of love for this small, appealing girl huddled into her raincoat — and knew, too, with a swift confidence that would not be denied that she cared for him . . . perhaps much more than he had dared to hope.

"Honor," he said gently. "Come and have some coffee, you're cold." And he took her hand in a very natural manner and led her across the road to Mike's Bar. He walked with her, feeling the cold, tight clasp of her fingers, conscious of the love that emanated between them as he looked down at her and felt happier than he had ever been in his life.

Whatever the future might hold for them both, he felt that they would be together, and Calder could want nothing more than to love her, to know her love and to be with her for the rest of time.

THE END

Other titles in the Linford Romance Library:

A YOUNG MAN'S FANCY
Nancy Bell

Six people get together for reasons of their own, and the result is one of misunderstanding, suspicion and mounting tension.

THE WISDOM OF LOVE
Janey Blair

Barbie meets Louis and receives flattering proposals, but her reawakened affection for Jonah develops into an overwhelming passion.

MIRAGE IN THE MOONLIGHT
Mandy Brown

En route to an island to be secretary to a multi-millionaire, Heather's stubborn loyalty to her former flatmate plunges her into a grim hazard.

WITH SOMEBODY ELSE
Theresa Charles

Rosamond sets off for Cornwall with Hugo to meet his family, blissfully unaware of the shocks in store for her.

A SUMMER FOR STRANGERS
Claire Hamilton

Because she had lost her job, her flat and she had no money, Tabitha agreed to pose as Adam's future wife although she believed the scheme to be deceitful and cruel.

VILLA OF SINGING WATER
Angela Petron

The disquieting incidents that occurred at the Vatican and the Colosseum did not trouble Jan at first, but then they became increasingly unpleasant and alarming.

DOCTOR NAPIER'S NURSE
Pauline Ash

When cousins Midge and Derry are entered as probationer nurses on the same day but at different hospitals they agree to exchange identities.

A GIRL LIKE JULIE
Louise Ellis

Caroline absolutely adored Hugh Barrington, but then Julie Crane came into their lives. Julie was the kind of girl who attracts men without even trying.

COUNTRY DOCTOR
Paula Lindsay

When Evan Richmond bought a practice in a remote country village he did not realise that a casual encounter would lead to the loss of his heart.

ENCORE
Helga Moray

Craig and Janet realise that their true happiness lies with each other, but it is only under traumatic circumstances that they can be reunited.

NICOLETTE
Ivy Preston

When Grant Alston came back into her life, Nicolette was faced with a dilemma. Should she follow the path of duty or the path of love?

THE GOLDEN PUMA
Margaret Way

Catherine's time was spent looking after her father's Queensland farm. But what life was there without David, who wasn't interested in her?

HOSPITAL BY THE LAKE
Anne Durham

Nurse Marguerite Ingleby was always ready to become personally involved with her patients, to the despair of Brian Field, the Senior Surgical Registrar, who loved her.

VALLEY OF CONFLICT
David Farrell

Isolated in a hostel in the French Alps, Ann Russell sees her fiancé being seduced by a young girl. Then comes the avalanche that imperils their lives.

NURSE'S CHOICE
Peggy Gaddis

A proposal of marriage from the incredibly handsome and wealthy Reagan was enough to upset any girl — and Brooke Martin was no exception.

A DANGEROUS MAN
Anne Goring

Photographer Polly Burton was on safari in Mombasa when she met enigmatic Leon Hammond. But unpredictability was the name of the game where Leon was concerned.

PRECIOUS INHERITANCE
Joan Moules

Karen's new life working for an authoress took her from Sussex to a foreign airstrip and a kidnapping; to a real life adventure as gripping as any in the books she typed.

VISION OF LOVE
Grace Richmond

When Kathy takes over the rundown country kennels she finds Stinton, a local vet, very helpful. But their friendship arouses bitter jealousy and a tragedy seems inevitable.